The Frenched Pearl

THE FRENCHED PEARL

Nine Short Stories of Erotica From the 21st Century

David Vercauteren

Kapowsin Publishing

Seattle, Washington, USA

Contents

Preface

There are many aspects of life that feature borders and restrictions that are designed to make everyone comfortable. The predictability of tomorrow, for example, is what defines and ensures social stability, as well as the room to dream freely. This book was written because the stability and predictability of American life provided to me, has functioned as a kind license with which to dream the dreams that need dreaming in our ever-changing country. I am an abstract artist, writer, and Marine, originally from the San Francisco Bay Area, but now living in Washington State.

Recently, several people have passed away who were within my life sphere who were only in their thirties and forties, immediately and tragically reminding me how short life and our time here on Earth and in our country, can be. It was then I decided to write this book, reflecting my engagement with exotic places, memorable times, and erotic fantasies. Along with the stories included here, you will also find abstract designs and a quote to conclude each story.

The inspiration for the book derives from my experience reflecting upon my memories, the most outstanding moments of my past that come back to me, for various reasons, voluntarily or involuntarily. At some point, the images I conjured became increasingly vivid to me, often everyday child experiences, like riding my bike to school in the autumn wind, jumping curbs, breathing deeply, and dodging branches. But I also found equally vivid memories emerging from not-so-everyday events that occurred throughout my young adulthood and middle-age. The mental snapshots of my erotic encounters – in particular when mixed with a dose of fantasy – serves as the grounding source for this book of exotic erotic stories. My circumstances dictated, of course, a list of alternatives and paths that I might take, or might not be able to. I ended up taking the more daring one, not being one to back down!

Here are some of the most lasting images that made an impression on me:

My father, when he was a young adult, was a greaser with the then oft-celebrated T-bird car, in the San Francisco Bay Area. At one point, driving wildly on the area roads, he ended up in a car crash in which he was ejected out of the car, and, yet somehow, still survived. He would then live his life, from that point forward (and ensuring that I knew it!), with the attitude, "Well, I'm not supposed to be here anyway." As if he cheated death, and that there's only one life to live, so let's get to it! His vibrant passion for existence and the adventurous, sometimes worrisome decisions he made in life served as a central source of inspiration for my own decision-making process.

On the female side of my family, my mother and grandmother also contributed a lot: they provided for me a sense of the beauty of a woman, the intuition of love, and the look and poise of confidence and decisiveness. They made me feel like I was capable of anything, always quick to give me a warm hug or knowing smile, to bolster my sense of standing as an individual. When they died, they both passed away within a year of one another, which, perhaps even more than the influence of my father, triggered me to try to understand the deep sense of emptiness that I felt inside. I was quite young at the time, yet even today, all these years later, I can still hear my mother screaming her support for me from the soccer field sidelines.

Searching for the real answers to all of my questions, I reflected over the course of one day for almost all of it, realizing the pain that came from the fact that now my mother was gone, my grandmother was gone, my dad was barely hanging on, and that my sister had, for her own reasons, also moved on. I felt completely empty, unsure of how to push further. Then, after these feelings emerged and took hold of my consciousness, I decided I needed a break. So I ordered a pizza and cherry cola and consoled myself with a comfort food-filled stomach. Later, in the cold evening, I lit candles at the dining room table, grabbed a pencil and a piece of paper, and truly let my emerging inner writer go to work on all of these thoughts and emotions.

I was surviving, deep in thought. I had lit the candles to warm my hands, as I didn't know how to work the thermostat at that age. I vividly remember the feeling of deep curiosity I felt and the drive to reflect more seriously upon my feelings than I ever had. Everything that has come to pass since I think, resided in that moment, a moment of rebirth and, I also like to imagine, of my own unique, inner "superpower." I mean, everything had been taken from me — but now, it seemed, I had discovered something different, something that no one could ever take. So, I became an abstract artist and a writer at the early age of twelve years old, all out of the realization of and confrontation with the hollowness that had been produced within me — it was one I knew I needed to fill, and I was determined to. My childhood family life was now gone, and new, more simplified, but more difficult chapters would follow, as I moved on through the world with only my father at my side.

During this period, I would change schools fifteen times, never developing true roots anywhere, and also, with my dad never really letting go. His most famous words, it seemed to me in reflection, were "Pack it up, son. We're moving!" Dad said he went to many schools when he was young and was popular at most of them. He thought it came from his attitude that, as he put it, "Hey, I'm not going to be here very long, anyway. No need to be too concerned with people's opinions. I'll just be myself." His sparkling blues eyes, long eyelashes, black hair, and unswayable confidence played the central part in how that played out, as did his design of what a man ought to be like. Needless to say, I took on the same attitude, partying through many of the high school years, even though this also meant my grades would take a massive hit. My dad wasn't particularly bothered. He would say, "Don't worry about it Dave, you're a great human being." I guess I just believed him and became a person who was always ready to move and discover new people and places, regardless of how well I was or wasn't doing.

Now in my teens, my grandfather, a gunsmith, would watch cowboy shows with me, and quiz me on the types of guns that were used. I would sit down next to him, usually giving a few right answers at least! One time I asked if he had any advice for me, to which he simply replied, "No." About ten minutes rolled by and suddenly, he spoke up: "Ok, yeah, I got some advice for you, don't miss out on your youth. Live every day as if it were your last, and David, embrace every moment as fully as you can." I took my grandpa's advice seriously, as it rang through my thoughts every day to try to understand what he meant. I don't know why, exactly, but I just thought his wisdom must be important! He's my dad's dad and a fine human being.

Well, working through all of this, I nevertheless managed to squeak through my young adult life despite having spent much of my high school being disciplined in juvenile hall. I got off a little easier than others, I guess because I was already enlisted to join the Marines. I was to be stationed in Hawaii where I'd be working day-in and day-out with heavy equipment. When I arrived, I learned the Commanding General had the same last name as I do, Vercauteren. So, I became a kind of semi-celebrity on the base due to my name tape, but I bet it was also because of everything I had learned from my family across my lifespan, the kind of individual that I was.

With my father's "I'm not supposed to be here" attitude, my mother's and grandmother's warmth and confidence, and my grandfathers' advice to not miss anything, I would engage the world in my early adulthood all on my own, doing as much as I possibly could in life, often landing me in places so romantic, exciting, dangerous, and unbelievable, that I really never could have guessed what would come. The Aloha spirit of Hawaii blessed me and really balanced everything out, validating all of my family's advice, love, and lifestyle. From there, I moved to Los Angeles; Carmel, Washington; San Francisco; New York; San Jose; and so many other locations that it seemed like it would be more or less endless.

After leaving the Marines, I met my wife in Santa Cruz, and after backpacking Italy, we became happily married. Still, though, that gnawing sense of emptiness persisted. I was confused why the world wasn't as bright and brilliant as I thought it was and also, why people weren't nearly as loving as I thought they were. All the same, she really kept me grounded and balanced. She too had her favorite saying, which would center my thoughts and mend my soul every time she said it: "It's not about you."

As you can probably tell, many different travels and experiences have marked me and remolded me in different ways, at various points throughout my life. During this day and age, with where America is at, I wish to impart upon my son, and also my readers, the central importance of civility, and I strongly hope he'll (and we'll) be able to experience it much more in the days to come than I did in my time. The further down the road we go, the more I realize how my art, my poems, my philosophies, and my patriotism, as forms of self-expression, and as forms of self-making and remaking, have all become more or less atypical, unlike in the past, when they were second nature to many of us.

We've lost something very important in our society, it seems. However, the freedom to boldly reflect my exploratory, thoughtful nature in a book of erotic stories is still within my power because, as my Dad always said, "I'm not supposed to be here anyway (so why not?)." Just as he could have died driving that T-bird so wildly many years ago, I too, could have died in combat or similarly dangerous situations. But I didn't, I survived.

The characters in this book then, are drawn from my life and that of others I've known, while the adventures derive similarly but not completely, from the places I discovered in the various corners of life. The stories are not meant to be read through all in one sitting. The story you choose on a particular day should be explored as you proceed into your day and your imagination begins to unfold in response. So, we'll take a look into forgotten, yet still lively desires and moments, and perhaps you will discover the sensation of the erotic where you least expected it. My hope is to inspire an openness to another perspective for adults who once knew these feelings and, also, those who yearn to discover erotica as it exists today, beyond the screen. The art and the philosophy are the salt and pepper I provide the reader after each story, or, alternately, the gari between delicious bites of sushi to refresh the palate anew.

1

Sinister

From her well-placed, yet modest apartment, Pearl was able to walk many places easily, to get the things she needed in her crowded section of Los Angeles. Sometimes, she enjoyed walks through the farmer's market to pick up her fresh fruits, vegetables, and goat milk soap. She loved the effusive lathering the soap provided and felt deeply sensual while caring for and cleaning herself in the shower.

One day, after a walk, she leaned back against the shower wall, her hands gliding down her slick body while she remembered her classes at church long ago.

There was a guy named Tommy who convinced her to leave the classroom and to meet her outside near the bushes. The vegetation was concealed from the older adults in the area, but easy to get through and to settle into the back. Pearl met him with excitement. He was clean-cut and much taller than Pearl. He pulled her arm into the open spot behind the bushes and put her hand on his penis.

"Stroke it!", he said, excitedly.

Confused and surprised, she pet his penis and was amazed at the firmness of Tommy's bulge. He unbuttoned his pants and told her to get on her knees. Tommy pulled it out of the underwear flap. For the first time, Pearl saw a male's private parts up close. With her eyes wide open, she steadily bent to her knees.

"Now kiss it."

"No!", Pearl said, disgusted.

"Come on."

"No".

"Then stroke it."

Pearl put her hands around Tommy's penis and began to stroke it gently. His eyes closed and his breathing got heavier and heavier.

"Spit on it"

"No", returned Pearl.

"Come on".

"No"

"Fine, I'll use my spit," Pearl sighed.

"Go ahead."

Feeling impatient, Tommy aimed his spit down to his penis, but his aim was less than stellar and Pearl got some on her hand. She noticed when she squeezed the head and tightened her grip, he would get very excited. It was also very slippery, which interested her, too. All the same, she began to get nervous.

"We have to go back."

"No we don't, we're not done," complained Tommy.

"Done with what?"

"You know."

"I'm going," said Pearl.

She stood up and walked out of the bushes while he pulled up his pants and followed her back into the school. For the next few days, the experience kept coming back to her, and she realized she enjoyed doing what she did in the bushes so much that she called and asked him to do it again the next Saturday. Tommy was surprised and giddy about the whole thing.

When the next Saturday arrived, they both snuck into the bushes again during class. This time, though, Pearl wanted to explore further what Tommy's definition of "done" might mean. She used her spit and with growing confidence, leaned into his penis, lightly touching his testicles. Overwhelmed with pleasure, Tommy jumped and came on her shirt and face – much to Pearl's surprise. Covered and fully ablush, she searched for something to clean up with. Tommy unbuttoned, took off his undershirt, and helped to clean her face. Pearl loved it, the attention, the sensation, the excitement. This became routine every Saturday and became more and more intense each time – to the point, even, that there were lubes and cushions already waiting for them in the bushes when they would come.

One hot Saturday morning, she met him at the bushes, but, a bit startled, realized that he was not alone.

"Who is this?"

"This is my friend Ben," said Tommy.

"Why is he here?"

"I told him how amazing you were and he begged me to come out here to see if you would..."

"Would what?" insisted Pearl.

"You know."

Pearl looked at the boy, who was suddenly overcome with a look of fright upon his face.

"Have you ever done this?" she asked him.

He shook his head.

"Well?" said Pearl, with a smile and a glance at his crotch.

Ben slowly undid his jeans and pulled his pants down to his underwear. Almost like she was made for this, Pearl pulled his underwear down further, caressing his legs. Unable to completely relax, he shook like a leaf. His erection was already engorged, presenting itself awkwardly, but prominently. Pearl realized that his penis wasn't all that much different than Tommy's, so she performed her stoking as she had at first, with Tommy.

"You can leave now Tommy."

"What? Why? This is my party," he protested.

With a smile from Pearl, Tommy pulled down his pants and told her to play with both of them at the same time. Pearl smiled at the challenge and with both hands, stroked both of them. Both closed their eyes as Pearl listened to them moan and slide their feet around in the dirt. Ben quickly became excited so she stroked him gently while tightening her grip on Tommy, taking longer strokes. She played this game back-and-forth between them until both were actually sweating, beet red in the face.

The wonder of control for Pearl was discovered at that moment. She thought to herself wryly, "Could I make them cum at the same time?" Ben started to leak precum as Pearl twisted her hand upon the head of his penis. Tommy, for his part, leaned back in ecstasy, but since she already knew to dodge his squirting cum antics, it merely landed upon the leaves. This experience, she would later realize, set the tone of her sexual life and struggles throughout the rest of her life.

Now older and living her own life in the same part of L.A. she grew up in, Pearl was the kind of woman who doesn't leave. But that also meant she witnessed the ways in which the neighborhoods changed over time. Nowadays, when Pearl arrived home from her job driving a school bus, there was often a young man booming his music so loud, she could feel the vibrations. Sometimes on her worst days, she would place him in a sinister light, taking out her anger on him internally to make sense of her day through a kind of emotional projection.

In fact, after it happened one too many times, Pearl began to see this young man as a modern-day advocate for Satan himself. On other days though, he seemed appealing, like possibly the kinkiest, rarest fruit of a man she could imagine, given how they would sometimes lock glances. Pearl was upset that management did nothing about the volume he imposed and she was too tired to go over to say anything after dealing with all the kids, parents, aids, teachers, and – especially in LA – bad drivers on the road all day. As she became older she no longer possessed the drive for confrontation that she once held in her younger years.

Pearl was thoughtful about it though, knowing that rumors could spread fast in the small apartment building they live in and her true colors could be in question if her truths were ever discovered. On not-so-tired days, she often felt a quick, playful flirt with her sexy neighbor would reveal her darker, more intimate side to him. Her fear of blushing her pale white skin, though, usually kept her from looking back when he was looking at her from the front balcony deck. Leaning around the palm trees to make eye contact and get her attention was more often than not, an effort to no avail.

As a now-older Christian woman, Pearl was unusual in that she harbored an extremely high sex drive, leading her to masturbate all the time. More than anything, she wanted to appear decent and prudent to her neighbors, friends, and family alike, so it was important to her to hide her horny inclinations. Deeper down though, the memories of her sexual escapades throughout life pervaded her thoughts, and little private spaces like the shower began to serve as important contexts within which she could release the tension. When Pearl was in the shower with her soaps and wall suction toys, there were literally no boundaries. Her fantasies ran deep, and her actions drew from her emotions, taking her down paths she never even imagined possible.

Sometimes afterward, Pearl would feel a sense of a return to innocence, of staying aligned with her definitions of love and humanity, despite her complicated erotic thoughts. Yet, it was a daily struggle. She would walk around a nervous wreck much of the time as a result, worried about her behavior and the dark reflection on her reputation that it might leave. As she saw it, love is increasingly untended to and unheard of in the mass media, such that her most inner fibers of being bristled at what she witnessed on an everyday basis.

One hot summer day, Pearl arrived at her apartment, noticing a flyer on the door: "Apartment Building Party-Appreciation for Residents this Saturday! Wear comfy clothes or PJs and relax. Starts at noon-bring your favorite dish."

Not thinking too much of it, Pearl wasn't sure what to wear except her summer shorts, or perhaps, leggings with her tie-dyed wolf's head T-shirt. The days had been warm recently, so she decided the shorts from working with girl scouts would be best – along with a quick trim to the bangs. Her work glasses seemed to her a bit dated, so she looked around to find her newer ones that, although they didn't work as well for seeing, might be more presentable for flirting. She also knew, of course, that this might help her find her way to the young flame of a man who kept trying to get her attention. Thinking of all the possibilities, Pearl stayed up late watching old black and white shows, leading her to pass out very late.

When Saturday arrived, the sun rays began to cross her closed eyelids, but Pearl just rolled over, falling into another sleep cycle. As soon as she did, though, she was woken up to a loud booming sound coming from outside. This time, it was from a car in the parking lot. "What's with all the noise?" she screamed, leaning over her window.

Annoyed, Pearl got up and looked at the clock: it was 12:30 pm. Her focus was suddenly upended. In a hurry, she jumped up, got ready, grabbed her ambrosia out of the refrigerator, and speed-walked to the party. She was determined to make the most of it.

On the way there though, she noticed the young music man leaning outside his front door on the rail, attempting to project a look of dourness and temptation to her. His tan, well-defined muscles were intoxicating to her. "He is irresistible to look at," she thought. Pearl was extremely nervous as she observed him talking to a tall clean-cut man, but she couldn't see his face clearly. With a whimsy of fantasy, she speculated to herself that perhaps the man he was talking to was actually Tommy, her first sexual partner.

"That better not be Tommy up there with him," Pearl thought.

A handsome devil, he squinted a bit when he looked down at her with his expensive clothes and poised sexy smile.

She tensed up. "He's so evil, he's so evil," Pearl repeated in her mind, grinding her jaw, just slightly.

A few weeks prior, when she had been complaining about the music man, she had learned from another neighbor that he was from Bordeaux, France originally, but had moved to LA to seek a career in film. She couldn't remember the name she had been told – "P.. P... ah, Pierre!" Triggered by the memory of Tommy though, who had left a mixed impression on her, she just speed-walked away, sighing in her worry, while hearing lingering laughs in the background.

By the time Pearl got to the pajama party though, most of the other tenants were already leaving or were deeply engaged in exclusive conversations in the TV room. The room seemed a little hot and sticky from the weather and combined with the number of people in there, it wasn't getting any less so. So Pearl put her ambrosia with the other food and took a bashful glance around her, with her hands folded behind her back.

With her bangs cut straight across and her silly style of-the-moment on full display, she feared no one would talk to her. That, of course, was the precise moment Pierre walked in wearing a ribbed tank top and soft PJ bottoms, adorned by copious flames that to her, seemed a bit ridiculous. As he headed straight for the food where Pearl was standing, she braced herself but smiled politely. His reckless air and looks of dishevelment amused her a bit, but she also sensed a potentially limitless well of mischief they might draw from in the future.

"Would you like to try my ambrosia?", asked Pearl.

Pierre looked up at her through his eyebrows, with just a touch of self-revelation: "Of course I would."

The flirting and the tight bond they would later fully develop began at that moment, and was totally electric. They both picked out a few items from the potluck, before Pearl, now emboldened, asked if he would like to join her at a small table against the wall. The atmosphere between them was one of wickedness and sin since they both knew that there was a bit of mutual enmity between them, and yet the attraction pulled upon them both all the more strongly as a result of it. Pierre's European gestures felt smooth and easy to be around for her, whereas, Pearl's gestures – fidgety, excited, and nervous – revealed the depth of her interest.

Rather than waiting for him to speak first, she struck up what amounted at first, to a nervous, shakey-voiced conversation with him. Unsure what to talk about exactly, Pearl brought up her son, which for him imputed a sense of vivaciousness and command that he had not expected. Pearl related to Pierre that she wanted her son to marry a good Christian wife who always did her daily prayers. Her compassion for youth and the changes they go through were apparent to Pierre, and his interest in her began to develop further.

Pearl, however, was still quite nervous and blurted out, "Ya know, they say Dopamine is stronger than heroin? Did you know that?"

Raising an eyebrow curiously, Pierre's heavy French accent intoned, "No I didn't know that."

"Cyber-bots are the wave of the future. We can't escape them you know," said Pearl.

"Cyber-bots?"

"Yes! Tribes have always been important and they still are today!"

Pierre smiled, reflecting on her passionate, yet odd opinions. Nevertheless, he was flattered that she had finally opened up to him, so he just sat there, gazing into her sparkling eyes, as Pearl went on-and-on about how she works in the community, and how she does the popcorn at the local high school basketball games, amongst many, many other things. For her too, the discussion functioned as a kind of evasion, hiding from the fact that she was totally mesmerized by him and couldn't stop looking at him. Pearl watched Pierre's face and expressions to try to get a read on his feelings, hoping and looking for a reflective response that would match her own. Alas, because he said so few words with his thick French accent, it was quite hard to tell.

So Pearl just talked about how many cyber-friends she had, bragging endlessly about it even though he gave her a polite, yet suspicious look of partial disbelief. Knowing that she was somewhat delusional and probably lonely, he felt pity for her but was also attracted, secretly. She sometimes got stuck in a verbal pause, while he just smiled at her, leaving her feeling a bit dumbfounded.

To Pierre, her condition seemed permanent, something she would struggle with for the rest of her life, while her transparent prudishness became more and more attractive to him, as they increasingly built trust over their conversation. It was clear to her that Pierre could relate to a lot of what she discussed – however, his strong sense of instinct revealed to him a more concealed reason, maybe even to her own consciousness, for her sweet, friendly expressions.

To pass the time, they told stories, shared their everyday lives, and became more and more familiar with one another. Pearl kept biting her tongue to stop her from mentioning the music being loud, something she wanted to mention but, since she also didn't want to alienate him in the process, she couldn't quite do. Pierre spoke about some failed relationships and events he had experienced, in particular his stage lighting job, which he hated. While in other contexts, this might have seemed insecure, for Pearl, it was a mark of honesty, and it only built her trust in him that much further.

From Pearl's vantage point, a fit, a link, a commonality, was readily apparent in the flourish of sexual tension they were slowly releasing to one another, as they drew closer and closer. While listening to his stories, her rejoinders that connected her life story with his thrilled her desire, and to a degree she had not expected. In fact, she had gotten to the point of not hearing him, or his French accent, at all. Pearl was too busy plotting in her mind how exactly, to seduce him. Her sex was dripping with anticipation to such a degree that she thought she had better go home, change her clothes, and come back to meet him again.

None of this was lost on Pierre, however. Observing her rising-and-falling dimples coupled with her cute smile, he used his French accent to address philosophy: "The real question is, how shall we live, right? What are we to do with our desires to make us happy once again?"

In a start, Pearl snapped out of her trance, where she had been imagining stroking him, making him smile at her shocked, yet pleased expression. Witnessing her weakness for him growing and her glow becoming radiant, Pierre understood that there wasn't a moment to lose. His attraction had obviously been exposed to her, and even while her anxieties remained, she was melting in his presence, right before Pierre's eyes.

Her momentum swept him up too, causing him to jump up in his pajamas and head outside of the party, so as to avoid embarrassment from his semi-erection. Humbled, and wanting to be polite, Pierre said to Pearl that he was going to go back to his apartment. Intrigued, and not yet ready to give up, she followed him a bit, asking if he likes loud music, in a bid to turn him on just a bit more than he already was.

Pierre chuckled, knowing the tone in her voice indicated a deeper yearning for an invitation to his apartment. She struggled between her desire and her faith every moment of their interaction, knowing how very un-Christian her motives technically were.

"Are you coming with me bus driver lady?", Pierre smiled back, handsomely.

Her eyes went aflutter in a way that she could not control, as her center began to bud and throb. Pearl's heart-wrung instincts were about to be released from the haunting fantasies of intimacy with him she had harbored, and to her, it felt world-shaking.

Her face was radiant with happiness as she followed Pierre to his apartment, looking around to see if anyone was noticing. The air was hot and the palm trees swayed. The old lady down the way looked over at the two with a raised eyebrow while carrying her laundry. Shaking her head, she disappeared around a corner, and Pearl and Pierre forgot about the incident as quickly as they'd been faced with it.

When the door shut behind her, she followed Pierre into the galley kitchen. Her nervousness caused her to lose her balance, falling to her knees just behind him. Looking up longingly, she caressed his legs and butt. Looking back, he grinned, enjoying her smooth, determined movements, so warm and tender.

"Don't talk", said Pierre.

Pearl's forceful assertion from behind had decided the destiny of her caressing motion. In his soft pajamas, Pierre felt a soft reach-around massage sending deep waves of pleasure to his member. He stiffened and moaned to the rhythm of her tightening hands, treasuring the feeling of her face upon his behind.

Pearl then turned him around, embracing him with a close hug while on her knees. His sex was now completely hard. She slowly rubbed her face onto the outline of his concealed penis, licking his flat stomach, and pulling his PJs down a little, before laying a light layer of kisses upon the head of his penis.

Her tongue was especially playful. He gently patted the top of her head and realized her need for affection from him was by now, long overdue in her mind. He understood, with a bit of surprise, that he would be completely willing to submit to her, as he pet her cheek and pulled his PJs to his knees. While rubbing his legs, Pearl's eyes suddenly opened in amazement and shock, upon running into his well-manicured package.

"It has been too long," she says.

Pierre flexed his sex for her and her nervousness melted, revealing something quite different: a wide-smiling, teeth-grinding, wild animal of a woman. The beast had been set loose! Pierre's manic laugh only intensified as she began to grunt and growl, clawing at his penis as they kissed, in a werewolf-like sexual mania.

It was at that moment that Pierre yelled, "wait! stop!!" Pearl was startled but relieved when he pulled his PJs up, walked over to his stereo, and turned the bass music up before closing the blinds. He turned off the main lights and, instead, turned on his pet snake's light, revealing the monster of a python he kept writhing inside a glass cage.

Getting the meaning of Pierre's physical metaphor, and without taking her eyes off of his erect sex, Pearl's breasts began heaving with desire, offering herself to his ritual. She stripped down without thinking, unabashed, drugged with the degree of her longing. Pearl's battles between her frigid politeness and her secret, obscene behaviors soon receded and she drank the cocktail of cravings deep: for emotional adventure, for physical quenching, and for an end to the turbulence in her heart.

Pearl's deprivation was about to be relieved. Throwing Pierre onto his back on the sofa, she whispered firmly, "Don't you move."

She stripped his PJ bottoms off, quivering with anticipation, as he sank into the sofa with a scoot and a slide. The room was very hot and drenched in a feeling of sin for sweet Pearl, whose beliefs had always weighed heavily upon her, however, always also with a degree of paradox. A thousand prayers to bear, and the anguish of these learned symbolic chains, restrained her no more. Sweating, Pearl jumped on top of him, which clapped their bodies audibly, before her glasses fell off. He braced himself with his feet and his arms on the sofa to stabilize himself.

The sensation of his skin on her body forced the blood through her heart, rapidly charging the moment. His rotating tongue on her nipple intensified her panting and tormented her flesh. She placed his stiff, thick sex inside her, with one leg on the ground, panting like a lioness at her power over him. In this temple of heat, bass, and the writhing, illuminated snake, Pearl issued a dozen hard, hot squeezes to conquer her runaway fantasies. With multiple expressions of joy and a relentlessly pulsating body, she tightened her inner lips, sucking him in as her moisture seeped out. In submissive admiration, he beheld her snarling, yet beautifully honest face, while approaching orgasm.

"Dear heavens no, oh no!"

Her quick and devilishly teary-eyed orgasm unleashed a pearly cascade of holy water unto her person. Shocked, Pierre was fixated on Pearl's facial expressions and her saliva, now drooling from the bottom of her mouth.

She slowly and steadily rode and tilted his erection deep down inside of her. Pierre could hold himself no more and came powerfully inside of Pearl, hard enough that she could feel the gush of his hot fluid bath. She lay on top of him, practically falling asleep, as she recalled her vows and ambitions of piety, despite giving way to her new erotic bouquet. Laying there heaving, she mentally sifted through her pent-up frustrations and cookie-cutter beliefs, realizing that she had little option other than to give in. As she did, a vision of white feathers fluttering in the air passed through her mind, leading her to feel she was able to really breathe, for the first time.

Without bathing, they both fell asleep, well into the late afternoon, with Pearl on top and Pierre inside, as he abided by her wishes. The two of them were one, marinating in the pulp of a fermented Pearl, while Pierre realized he had indeed, found a permanent place in his heart for her.

"Those who always do good in their lives, live good lives. Those who do a little bit of bad, live better ones" (DRV)

2

The Play Ride

He had been out of the Marines for ten years, leaving him with little money to live on. But one day, out of nowhere, Charlie received a will of money and property from his estranged father, an inventor of airplane parts. He was living on the east coast when his father passed away. Though his Dad was a born genius and won many awards, he was unsuccessful with creating lasting relationships, including with his own offspring.

Charlie was his father's only son and left him his whole estate which included International Patents, Trademarks, Copyrights, Stocks, Bonds, the houses, and all the electronic gadgets and toys he had collected. Relatives he didn't know began to call the house and Charlie began looking for ways to dodge them, since he really didn't know them in the first place. Charlie received invitations to the wake and funeral, but declined, he felt, out of respect. Charlie and his Dad's bumpy past had practically burned a hole in his heart and moving away seemed like the best way to bury the memories of their many knockdown, drag-out fights.

A few weeks after he did, Charlie received a message from his old Marine friend Fred, asking him to come out to celebrate the holidays. He had always been a good friend, even long-distance and for extended amounts of time. Fred had a horrible weakness for beautiful, young, misunderstood girls, the kind that simply liked to have fun. He'd always tried to be there for them when things would get rough: the night club type of guy who should probably have had a club of his own, with his flashy clothes and, typically, the most exotic, classy shoes. You'd never see Fred without a close shave and his hair done perfectly. In many respects, his friends would joke, he looked like a gigolo.

Agreeing to see him, shortly afterward, Charlie flew out to see Fred and found out that right after landing they would be going immediately to a Christmas Party with his parents and a bunch of their friends at a beautiful home in Southampton, New York.

"I'm not really dressed for a party Fred. The hoodie-jeans look isn't really what I want to wear."

"No worries, these people are old, stubborn, and stiff. They won't care what you look like anyway!"

As they arrived, Charlie observed the entrance gates to the property and the groomed branches and bushes. The pebbled driveway was luxurious which gave the house an even stronger sense of value and presence. They pulled up to the front of the house and parked by the nude sculpture fountain. Fascinated, Fred thrilled at his luck to be at the house, since it also was his first time there.

"Look at this place Charlie."

"Wow, yeah, real nice taste."

"Hope they have drinks inside."

"I bet they do!"

When they entered through the front door, Charlie immediately noticed that the men were all in khakis and sweaters. He felt as though he had entered into the conservative, distinguished air of well-heeled families who had been that way for generations, and as if they were turning their noses up at him as he entered the room. His working-class California swag immediately got their attention.

Defiantly, Fred smiled and whispered to Charlie, "Money can make a poor person."

Charlie smiled back but looked away, waving at the men without judgment.

"Hello everybody!"

Smiling still, he turned to Fred,

"We're smoking a joint later, devil dog."

Charlie gathered that Fred was not fond of their breed as they made their way towards the cherrywood bar. Predictably, the women were in the kitchen and the men were in the living room near the fireplace. Charlie and Fred were close enough to slow down their walk to the bar, but in this context, not enough to engage. The men continued talk of scandal and venomous enemies with the drunken, confident loudness of the wealthy. Yet, Charlie was tired from his flight and really wasn't interested in engaging in such nonsense. Charlie asked Fred to point him to the drinks so he could relax.

Charlie replied, while sipping his high-end whiskey, "I'm glad I came."

"Me too, I can't wait to show you around."

"Where are your parents?"

"Who the hell knows? They're probably in a fight about coffee creamer."

They both laughed.

Just then, Fred got a call from one of his girlfriends needing help in the city. He explained that he would be right back and not to worry. He wanted Charlie to stay at the house and eat, relax, put his feet up, while he fumbled through the night. Charlie agreed and listened in on the men and their bloated, blowhard statements, while Fred, growing sick of it, headed for the door.

Charlie was a young, handsome, benevolent, yet dark man, who had recently moved to Carmel, CA to receive his inheritance. Clearly a Republican room, he felt discarded by these rich, older men for being different from them. Even though he felt uncomfortable, Charlie sat quietly, as he just wanted to smile and listen while the men got smashed on gin and cognac. He sat in the old, red leather chair that he had admired when he walked in.

"Hey there Charlie, you better be a Republican in this house, or you're liable to get your ass kicked!" Laughter ensued.

"What does it matter? We just met."

"We want to know if you are one of the good guys or one of the bad guys."

Charlie's demeanor attracted more laughter and got the full attention of the room while he sat with his legs crossed and exhibited a controlled demeanor. He put his head down, feeling the burning in his stomach, up to his chest. He nervously rubbed his chest while they watched on and laughed.

With a firmness, one of the men said,

"Tough room isn't it, Charlie? What are you doing here? Fred bring you here?"

"Ya know friend, let me say one thing here — it's unpatriotic to put Politics over Civics".

"What do you mean, son?"

"Civics is about how we treat each other, whereas politics is about the powers that control the rules. I'm surprised you didn't know that, you should be cooler to people."

The wife of the house heard the last part of what Charlie said and winced, knowing he was about to get his head cut off.

"Dull, dull, dull you guys. Why don't you have this discussion in Burt's study so he can show you his trophies?"

In a flirty manner, she put her arm through Charlie's arm and said, "You can stay with me, let's go chat."

She pulled him into the kitchen and jumped up on the counter, revealing the shape of her body in her now-tightened dress.

"Where did you say you're from Charlie boy?"

"I'm currently living in Carmel right now."

He never spoke of his money and simply played along, enjoying, secretly, the underestimating comments he picked up with respect to his wealth. The wives were in the tea room, adjacent to the kitchen, but they couldn't quite see them. There was a tone of true flirtation as she sat on the counter, opening her legs to discreetly show her white panties. Charlie felt that she was out of his league with her majestic feminine stature, but she didn't think the same. In fact, he was refreshing to her, strange, attractive, and somewhat cornered in the unfamiliar context. He listened to the women talk as they eyeballed him up and down, like jaguars in heat.

She walked past him and whispered, "do you know how to light a furnace?"

He could smell her perfume and felt the air move silently past her. She watched him go into the tea room to snack on some food, with naughty thoughts on her mind.

She whispered as she glided by and touched his shoulder, "Want privacy?"

"With all my heart."

Her spirit felt blessed that it could now express itself. Her hands slid down his back to his behind, caressing. He knew he could show her a world of wonder and unfamiliarity, as he showed off his small, undulating tongue ring.

She whispered straight into his ear, as the women looked on quietly, "I know this a surprise, young man. But lust is powerful"

Her foreshadowings were acutely appropriate to his air of arousal. Her lips lightly touched his ear, as a sense of fear and caution filled the room.

"We are going to get so busted."

Without no worry on her face, she held a torch out to cast the light as she quickly left the room, heading for Burt's study. "Burt! I forgot something at the store, I will be back soon."

With her short, slim legs she grabbed her keys and motioned Charlie to follow her for a quick store run. Charlie knew they were was more too it, since they were weaving a dense net of flirtation, but could see no predictable path arising from it. She was intense, and he had no idea where they were headed.

At the store, she bought whip cream and cherries, making a confession in the store about her true feelings about Burt and his friends. She painted a domestic picture of her day-to-day and what damage it did to her spiritually, all while playfully dancing in the store, precisely to undo it all and start once more.

"Burt never goes down on me. It has been years since I've gotten any head," she said.

Charlie was flattered she was so open with him, so he expressed himself to her with a warm smile and a show of his tongue-ring, a kind of risque invitation. She closed her eyes, smile a bit, and breathed in a deep breath.

Charlie was intoxicated by her beauty and small stature. He was trying to control his erection while she teased him throughout the store with her cleavage and playing with different kinds of fruits, making him laugh and smile at her.

When they got back into the SUV, she pulled into the far side of the lot.

"What are we doing here?"

"Let me show you."

She pulled the can of whip cream out, asking him to lick the cream off of her finger with his tongue. Charlie played along, knowing her true inclinations were already brewing, deep in her sex. The cream shot onto her hand at first, then up her arm, next her neck, and finally, to her mouth. Her unsettled heart, she suddenly realized, had discovered a parting in the fabric of her reality, through which she could be free. Charlie was so dazed he didn't think much of anything except her, though the thought lingered that Fred was about to create a terrible mess for himself.

Charlie unbuttoned his pants and placed her hand on his member. Shocked that her hand was on his sex, she struggled, but she was immediately seduced because his dick was so much harder than Burt's and shaped differently too, in a way she knew would blow her mind. With the moment in blossom, there was nothing to do but submit to the wrong, which at least sometimes, can be deeply right. Their mutual desire had been ignited.

They climbed into the back seat and grabbed a beach blanket from the back.

"Now," she said, "Obey."

She slid onto her back, took off her panties, and placed the can of whip cream onto her drooling sex, with legs held high.

"Do you need practice Charlie?"

Charlie began to breathe heavily. He tossed the can and slowly bent down to savor her person. She watched as his mouth melted into the center between her legs, moaning the sounds he had so desired to hear. She wanted to be playful with him, but since his tongue was extremely long, it was actually he who surprised her. He pushed his whole tongue inside her, curling, twisting, thrusting his talent, producing a generalized mood of healing passion. Her private fulfillments were boiling over, swallowed up as they were, by his mouth.

The condensation on the windows eclipsed their everyday worlds such that it became their own private sanctuary of lust. He pulled her onto her upper back and pushed her legs back farther. His tongue ventured slowly beneath her sex and over the perineum. She couldn't breathe as his lips began to kiss her virgin anus, awakening it. Her pleasured nerves flickered and twitched as his skilled movements seemed to flow naturally, partially because he proceeded so gradually. She felt so taboo engaging in this affair and yet so sweetly released from her estranged loneliness, which had lasted far too long. Slowly, he tapped into her behind with his tongue, and then, without warning, all of his tongue went inside her. She moaned a loud, primal moan. She thought it would hurt to have something in her behind, but it didn't hurt at all. The longer he licked, the more it appeased her fears with growing pleasure, instead. She rubbed her eyes in disbelief and begins to rub her clitoris, in a hurry to achieve orgasm. He reached up to caress her breasts and teased her nipples.

Car lights beamed through the windows, exciting the series of repeated swirls, as if they were in some illicit dance club. He redoubled his tongue back and forth onto her sex with rhythmic talent and flawless intuition. A flowing beauty of the tongue and the face, his motions were laced with a timeless perfection. The steady repetition boiled over with pressure, as she squeezed his head with her legs and a small stream of delight splashed onto his face. She lightly fainted in the vibrant harmony and became a slave to his incessantly dabbing, long, powerful tongue, as it left its final sweet caresses for the night. He adored her.

"The adventure of life is a conscious forward effort to create joy and excite the soul out of its comfort zone" (DRV)

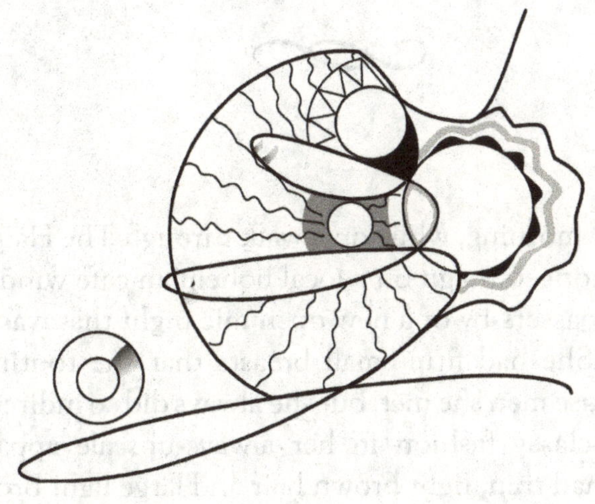

3

Oil!

One foggy morning, while on a walk through The Haight, Danielle noticed a sign on a local bohemian cafe window, notifying passers-by of a new open mic night that was set to begin. She had firm small breasts that she routinely used to rouse men she met, but she always did so indirectly and in a classy fashion in her always-upscale apparel. Danielle had thin, light brown hair and large light brown eyes, all of which was paired with an alluring, slightly raspy girl's voice. She loved to do open mics because she was able to communicate her poems more three-dimensionally than they would be in print, so as to mesmerize the room into a multitude of secret worlds of fantasy. She was sweet, curious, thoughtful, and also hopeful that at some point, she'd meet a decent and similarly poetically-minded man. Finding a man of passion with a heart that was true and pure seemed difficult to find, and not only because they can be so rare, but because her mind was constantly distracted by all of her ongoing problems. Exuding confidence, Danielle typically tried to hide how badly she needed the connection and how important to her the intensity of the moment must be.

The night of the first open mic, Danielle had dressed up in a sleeveless black dress with delicate makeup, heading to the café for a night of passion and sharing. In the back of her mind, she hoped that the elusive man she so desired would be in the room. She was trying to master reality with her yearnings, when, in reality, the deepest nature of a given moment is almost always unknown. The café was packed with San Franciscans and their creative, luminous air. Adorning the walls were large photos of the Grateful Dead, Carlos Santana, Martin Yan, Bruce Lee, Francis Coppola, Metallica, and more. Each of them were "behind-the-scenes" type photos, taken by those associated with venue, and were neatly matted and framed. The tapestry hangings were brilliant in color and woven perfectly. While gazing at the plants and lights, a man glided by exuding an air of leisure and elegance.

At first glimpse, he seemed as if he might harbor a somewhat tainted soul, but the truth of his world resided in his eyes, his presence, and his air, which she slowly understood. His clothes didn't seem to be important at all to him, yet he was elegant in presentation, all the same

Pascal found his way to the microphone with his blue jeans and plaid shirt, reading with a certain ferocity:

"The more I push, the rougher the road gets,
Pain, pain, within the brain,
I would like to show you my guiding light
And fleeting truths,
(moving his eyes around the room)

Make me a resident of my own free spirit,
Be proud to admit you were seduced by the cult of
dopamine.
So here's a toast, a tribute to our carousel lives,
Just guess, just guess, just guess which mask is next,
Snap? Series of heart attacks, hacks, tacks to where my
blood may fall,
Take a bath in my secrets or don't take one at all,
Now seemly enough, Love can't behave,
Oh please, oh please, oh please my Love,
Oh when will we be saved..."

Danielle could not believe the beauty of the words that
had graced her ears, nor the deep presence of his vocality.
Her eyes welled up with tears, though she was not
prepared for them. He was not looking down at a piece of
paper, but knew every line by heart. He knew his poem
as if he were from another time, another country, another
life. She thought, "Is he the one, the one I'm supposed to
meet?"

"Go ahead, you laugh and see the humor in all,
And when all is serious, pray to laugh,
Fear has a sick sense of humor,
Tucked away in his pocket,
And when the pocket is full,
I will fight and fight and fight,
Until my fists bleed of honor,
I love beyond the limits of earth and sky,
Your skin, your neck, your breasts,
You are a shade of gold,
As gold as the sky on a dusky beach ride,
I'll attune my empathy to your being and
kiss you over and over,
(His voice rose loudly)

But as I embrace you, feeling the coldness of your refrigerated heart,
It's as if I were surrounded by a cold damp mist,
Rub your hands together and hold your heart,
For your blood pump hibernates year-round,
All I hear is the thunder that roars inside my heart,
My head, I'm dead,
The cliffs of life are too steep for me to stand upon for you.
Deeply I stare into the darkness,
Into my workshop with confused angels and repeating voices,
The thicket of butterflies are taunting me,
My mind chatters, scatters, batters at the heart,
Hoping I will never be as lonely as a stray alley feline,
Go outside and talk to the golden tulips,
And ask them what we need to know,
Because in the glow, an endless glow,
Our souls will know what rose will grow.
Silence is my fear of which I'm giving to you.
Fulfill your prophecy and pilot yourself to the sun."

Applause broke out and Danielle made her way up to the poet. Pascal has his head down and was walking out with his hands in his pockets to the side of the café around the crowd. She tried to make eye contact, but he was moving too quickly through the crowd. She saw the top of the front door open and close, but couldn't get through the loudly clapping crowd without seeming rude. Fumbling, Danielle tripped over a support dog and dropped her binder. Surprised and worried that she wouldn't be able to get outside in time, she apologized to the man and dog, dusted herself off, and headed for the door. She saw him crossing the street in the light beams and ran towards the corner of the block, trying not to lose sight of him. She cried, "Stop! Wait!" Pascal heard her and halted. She was running in heels and fell a couple of times, making Pascal laugh. She finally caught up to him breathless and scared that he would think she was insane.

With a sweetly tilted head Danielle enquired boldly, "Did you forget something in the café?"

Pascal smiled and says "Did I?"

"Yes.... me"

"You?"

"Yes"

She caught her breath and again stated confidently, "me."

He smiled at her as they began their early evening walk, in which a connection emerged that felt as if had literally shaken the earth to its core. Looking over at her face, he realized how natural and easy it was for her to laugh at herself. She asked him if he had ever seen *I Love Lucy*. He smiled at the reference. "Oh the shine, the shine, the shine," he thought. "Ain't nobody going to dim this new shine."

On their downtown walk, they exchanged compliments, ideas, and love sonnets, while acting, walking backwards and forwards, leaping onto curbs, spinning on street poles, and dancing up staircases. Momentarily transported to a more youthful time, Danielle and Pascal disassembled the tall walls of prudishness together. They were polite to each other, paired with their respectful manners and hearts of compassion and adventure.

They paused in front of an art gallery and read a large painted sign that had been hung there, standing side by side. The reflection of the window teased them with a glimpse of themselves as a couple. While looking up at the large painting in the front window, she read a section of a poem that was painted on the canvas;

Stare into the flame of freedom,
Instead of the screen of blank,
Venture into the smell of Love or,
The mind will play the heart's prank.

Unaware of the time at this point, and now even more hopeful about their future, she imagined God's breath of destiny blowing through, intoxicating them both, so as to seal the reality of her wish and dream. The night grew colder and, since she had been so forward already, he asked her if she wanted to warm up with him and some wine he had to share at his studio. The night grew later and later as they carried on, the laughter leaving them in stitches, the wine in their veins further and further coaxing her wishes that much closer to reality.

The studio had a double function, as it was also his own private gallery of art, sculptures, tapestries, and fountains. The ceiling was high and his plants were mature. The large skylights and stained glass were contemporary and prismatic. But a stainless steel sculpture on the wall was the real eye-catcher.

Danielle asked, "What is that?"

"It is called:

Create a New World, With Wisdom Riding Shotgun"

"What about that other one over there?"

"That one is:

The Key Isn't Always to be Briliiant,

But to Find the Brilliance of Others"

"What about the one with the woman?

"I believe that one is:

The Cha-Cha flame of lust always starts with trust."

Pascal excused himself to the bathroom, but the mirror on the door was angled such that she could still see him slightly. Although Danielle could only barely see him in the reflection, her curiosity got the best of her and she leaned in to see him unbuckling his pants. His enormous circumcised sex fell towards the ground, leaving her in a state of disbelief and wonder. Her eyes grew as wide as dollars. She was nervous and looked away quickly, awakened, her body immediately succumbing to full arousal.

She said to herself, "Well, it's not his fault he's huge. Let's see what this is like."

She begins to snicker at her reckless self-talk. The desire and passion of two artists and poets was finally open and present, but now she was nervous as well as astonished by his sex. She began to realize just how in favor of his wild, dangling sin she was becoming as her nipples hardened. She wished so badly to be close to him.

As they chatted later, Danielle never mentioned she was newly divorced and Pascal never asked. She had mentioned one old relationship but didn't share the entire truth about it when she did, because she was so enraptured by him.

He waved and guided her to the alcohol in the kitchen, grabbing a glass and ice.

"And here you are," he said.

Danielle's dress was fashionable. She moved with a nonchalance toward him and slid his arms around her waist, moving his hands gently down to her brand new stockings, immediately swelling his heart. He was breathless as she turned around.

He guided her hands to his arms and moved closer, standing behind her at the chopping block in the kitchen.

He began kissing her cheek and necking her slowly, trying to catch his breath. His mouth was soft and patient. She tried to hold him around the waist with her arms behind his back, but she accidentally brushed her hand across his huge sex. She was surprised he didn't react. Her body bubble was immediately broken as he tongued her neck, lightly gripping her brown hair. She entered a state of erotic anguish and turned towards him. His pants strings were knotted tight and she was having trouble untying them. He didn't help, however, as he was enjoying her desire. She knew he would be thick, and could not wait to get directly to it.

Impelled by curiosity and laughing, he moved away with a pleasant smile, quickly making some food, opening a bottle of wine, and dancing to a pleasant beat. Danielle had longed for physical connection and hoped her nervousness didn't boil over into a perceptible state, thereby making him uncomfortable, somehow.

Missing her touch from a few moments before, he sneaked around the back of Danielle and tenderly laid his hands on her shoulders. He kissed and tongued her neck again. While slow dancing, his engorged erection began sliding and thumping her body, tempting her across the veneer of her dress, reducing her to a near slave to his hunger. His inflamed eyes, to her, spoke truth and, like her, he was also shameless. She uncontrollably wet her panties, due to a remainder of reluctance. She doubted herself, yet all the same, still harbored fleeting thoughts of holding his large sex firmly between both hands. He reached down towards her behind and assessed the proportions steadily.

"Is this ok?" She nodded and put his hand between her legs.

"I feel tortured"

"Well then, I'm truly sorry," he said with a smile.

He grabbed her arm and hand and placed it on his sex with great sensitivity and agility. Danielle bit her lip and slowly dropped to her knees, realizing she had acquired a new license to more freely explore. Feeling him more confidently now with her fingers, she was excited at the powerful shape of his sex that she could feel through his pants. She calmed down and gazed up at him, bearing eyes of neglect and longing. His hand shooka with anticipation as he maneuvered his sex through his pants slowly enough to thoroughly entice. Excited, she tried again to undo Pascal's pants, but they would not give way.

Danielle found her way to his bedroom, beckoning him to follow with a feminine, delicate walk on the tips of her toes. Poised at the foot of his canopied bed of fur, she waved him over with a playful smile, the throbbing feeling now completely unrelenting, between her legs. He turned on the electric fireplace in the room and smiled with an air of confident seduction. Passionately aware of her desire, he discarded his clothes, so as to reward her. Pascal slowly walked into the room naked, and then, remembering the one last thing he wanted to do before proceeding, he turned around, moving to the dresser where he kept his special raspberry-flavored oil, which he rubbed thoroughly and slowly, all over his body. He glistened in the light of the fire, while Danielle watched him do so, sitting with rapt attention on the bed. He moved closer to her. She was hypnotized, savoring the moment and the images. He started to massage his sex, enjoying the effect of his motions upon himself, and teasing her desirous mouth.

He said, "Do not speak a word."

She clung to every single second, almost dying in anticipation for the waiting to be over. He stood her up and turned her around again, placing a blindfold over her eyes and kissing her neck, over, and over, and over. Her dress has not been touched by him yet, and she did not take in his penis all at once, but savored the unfolding as it proceeded. Lightly licking his tongue on her bare shoulders, she curled her toes uncontrollably. Danielle witnessed almost-visible illusions of flower gardens as he ran a rose underneath her nose. She reached behind her but he was already in front of her. He kissed her face and her lips. She reached for him again, but he was already behind her now, sliding two fingers between her legs, expectantly. Her erotically intoxicated state had left her a bit delirious.

His raging, thick penis glazed her smooth legs before effortlessly massaging her sex through her panties. She laughed with pleasure until he moved her around and she felt his sex up against her behind, leaving her breathless and impassioned instead. Pascal lightly grabbed a large section of her hair at the root, asking permission to take off her clothes for her. He undressed her slowly with his eyes cast upon her body. Already having nodded yes, she mouthed "no" while laughing devilishly. He lightly spanked her with his big cock and took off her top. She smiled uncontrolably. Sweating in the now-hot room, she nervously pulled up her dress and pulled down her stockings and panties, bending herself over the bed. She could not quite define the state of mind she was in, having been so deprived for so long. There was no compass to guide her through her confounding conjunction of nervousness and arousal. Yet, the deepest parts of Danielle were already falling madly in love with the imagined life she knew she would be able to have with Pascal. She was paradoxically paralyzed by her stirred soul.

He then rubbed her vagina lips with his sex as she reached down to play with both. At first, she struggled with his erotic enthrallment, but as she slowly studied his small movements and gentle pressures, she gave in more and more to his will as it became inseparable from her own. Pascal smiled and enveloped her into a firm yet graceful and soft caress, from behind. He barely fit her, as their combined sweat conducted a deep friction and produced a relaxing massage. Between them, they produced a sacred time and place for one another, as she gazed into the large abstract paintings that he had on the wall. Danielle pushed back onto his sex, whispering "mmm yeah" to herself, as she did.

In a daze, she had finally reached the edge of the coming relief. Passionately, but with a loving sweetness, she rubbed her clit and reached under it for his giant, swinging testicles. She pulled out her tear-drop breasts to let them breathe in the moment of resonance. Pascal adored her faint cries of gratitude and the evidence of the slight pains she happily endured so as to submit to this inimitable moment. He was careful with both her mind and her body, changing positions over and over to see what position worked best for her. Twisting her person with care, he French-kissed the front and underside of her breasts. He was delicate with her nipples, albeit combined with an intentionally sloppy suction movement. Slightly stretched by him, her alpha side revealed itself animalistically as she forcefully pushed back onto him, deeper and deeper. At first Pascal was confused by the reversal – that is, until he saw the look of boundless ambition on her face.

She knew her buttons were going to be pushed in this moment of deep sensations, which made him vibrate uncontrollably. His reverberations excited her, since she knew the feelings she had were mutual. The pace quickened until she felt a warm, slow gushing, as she gazed entranced into the fireplace, pinching the head of his penis tightly with her vagina. Pascal hugged her and pulled her down onto it as their slickened bodies slithered in a lustful, moving caress.

"I love you Pascal."

He walked into the bathroom and cleaned her with a warm hand towel. After dressing, she was overcome by a sense of panicked frenzy, reaching down to pick up her panties and stockings and bolting out the front door. She stopped though, knowing he would see her condition, and smiled and waved. The door closed and once she was around the corner, a dizziness came over her as she spun to the ground, leaning against the wall, suddenly in a stream of unexpected tears. She thanked him with profound sincerity for the night in a whisper that he would not hear. It was the first night that she was baptized by her gigantic desire, leaving her a panting, changed spirit. She knew she would be back, following irrepressible yearnings just as Pascal knew he must wait for her to whisk him away again when she was ready, with her warm voice, her lovely poems, her expressive art, her penetrative ideas. They both knew the intensity and synchronization of their infatuation with one another was the formula for a new, deeply artistic resonance between them.

"Sexual gambling is timeless, Sexual risks are timeless,
An energy within us, From a tiny spark to a blazing torch."
(DRV)

4

Sneak Attack

Tina had never had writer's block before, but one day it finally hit, and she couldn't believe it. Tina lived in a small light-blue cottage in an upscale area with her roommate. Her hopes had been to someday meet the man of her dreams, but she had become frustrated waiting for him to spring into her life and whisk her away.

Her roommate Tabby was strikingly beautiful and had a reputation for being a little loose, with respect to sex. She grew marijuana in her living room, on the side of the house which got lots of sun. She was forever talking about her thick patches of leaves covered in crystals, the various shades of colors, and the rich, skunky smell her plants produced. The smell filled the entire cottage, but Tina didn't mind. She loved the smell.

Sometimes though, she got upset at her roommate for making dating look so easy. They were both small, thin, dirty blonde-haired ladies with rosy cheeks. They both liked to go tanning, to work out, to view art, and they both came from well-to-do families. Tina's hang-up was that she tended to get upset that she never got fully satisfied sexually, which was mostly because she was shy and not completely relaxed. But Tabby would just state jokingly, in her Aunt's Texan accent, "too pure for sinister attractions, ya prude!"

Tina went to college in Southern California and had a boyfriend there for a longtime. She had thought he was going to be the one, but her mother disapproved of his non-career-oriented mindset and made things difficult for the two pretty much every step of the way. Tina's mother had her ideal of what type of man would fit best into her family, even though her boyfriend constantly did the most romantic things imaginable for her daughter.

In those days, Tina and her boyfriend would go out on hikes and make love together deep in the middle of nature, or go to the beach and make love in various caves along the California coast. She missed those days very much, now.

To transcend her writer's block, she set out one warm afternoon at Point Lobos in Carmel for a hike, thinking that unplugging from the many technological screens she was always in front of would serve as a point of inspiration. Almost right away, two young men passed by and flirted with her, but Tina just immediately picked the men apart in her mind, thinking, "Surely there must be something really messed up about them." In the haze of her longing memories for her boyfriend, she had developed a sense of coldness and restraint, even to those who meant well and would never harm anyone. Her extreme anxiety over the dangers of being vulnerable had become debilitating, and it had very little to do with Tabby, even if she thought it did.

Tina hiked the sandy trail, watching the waves through the canopied cypress tree forest. She found a small trail that lead to a secluded cliff overlooking the ocean, which she was pleased to find featured a conveniently-placed wooden bench. As she sat upon it and looked outward, she realized her beauty, her dreams, and her reveries of the past had all dissolved into an unforeseen loneliness. What she didn't realize is that, as she recalled the past before this majestic scene, her hand had spontaneously ventured down the front of her shorts!

Her chronic starvation for touch had reached new levels that even she was unaware of. She realized that the screens she is consistently in front of probably played a major role in preventing a new romance from developing. As she braided her emotional fantasies and hopes for the future with her dramatized, idealized memories from the past, her fingers brought her to climax. She must love herself, she realized. She simply must.

Vivid thoughts of her anger toward her roommate, and how she had made Tina jealous to the core, caused her to realize she was unwittingly changing into someone she didn't know, and didn't want to be.

Whimsically, she asked herself out loud, "Should I just pursue purely physical relationships instead?" As she dipped her head back and rolled her hand faster in her shorts, she suddenly heard from behind her, "I think you found the best view in the park. These seas run deep."

She pulled her hand out of her unbuttoned shorts and started to get up. "Please don't leave," the tannish, good-looking man said.

Tina felt like running away out of embarrassment but seeing his calm and sweet face stopped her. David was a delicate type of gentleman from Spain and had a soft nature about him. His polished, intentional spirit and clean appearance piqued her curiosity. His skin was luminous and smelled faintly of cigarette smoke. As she grew more comfortable, he slowly sat down next to her as a magnetic and warm atmosphere of interaction emerged between them. They engaged in a flirtatious conversation about their memories of Big Sur and Paso Robles while sitting on the bench together, creating an unexpectedly strong vibration. As the conversation unfolded, they discovered she actually lived quite close to his brother's house in Carmel Valley. Her modesty and straight-talking truth was attractive to him, while he also noticed, to his pleasure, that she had never buttoned her pants back up.

Seeing all of this, he mentioned he was going to go see an old movie in a small theater in town and that if she'd like to, she would be welcome to join him. Tina politely declined. In the back of her mind though, she ventured into a fantasy about him, as many possibilities were clearly within reach. Not wanting to lose touch with her, he mentioned that he was also meeting some friends for wine and cheese at a nice restaurant downtown. Again, he asked Tina if she would join him. She wondered at that point whether he might actually be the piece of the puzzle she was missing and if she should simply say yes. He could easily see through her indecisiveness since although he was initially rejected, they were still marked by the unhidable symptoms of yearning. She was leaving no doubt that one of his offers to meet would be met with a positive response since the look in her eyes suggested a degree of taunting.

In the end, Tina agreed and followed David to the restaurant where they were left alone. The wine flowed easily and the air between them became sweeter and more fun, at once. Tina's silly jokes repeatedly had him in stitches, and he thanked her for the good laughs. At the same time, he felt a tingling in his core every time she would bat her sea-green eyes at him. He worried though, that she would notice his weakness.

So David changed the subject, going into extensivea detail about the fine grapes available in the area and how they were used in Napa Valley. He inspired her with his extensive knowledge and exuberant descriptions. She noticed though, that he was slowly talking faster and become more and more excited about her. Boldly, she kissed him on the cheek and wrote in a kind of scribbling on a napkin, "Thank you". The whole time, she had been developing a rather fetishistic desire to not only kiss him sweetly, but to quite frankly, straddle his face.

As they continued talking, she implied that her roommate would not be home and that, if they both wanted, the evening could be private unto themselves, and no doubt, rather exciting. The alcohol had produced a strong dose of courage that was also built upon a mutual awareness of the bond that had developed between them. David's sex suddenly thickened at the thought of this and he became quiet for the very first time since they'd met. He wrote on the same napkin she had written on, "Kiss me and we'll go." Tina stood up from her chair and slowly leaned down to kiss his lips. The soft kiss was filled with promise for both of them.

"Do you hear that? I believe my friends have arrived."

Suddenly, a booming sound reverberated from the alley behind the restaurant. David grabbed Tina's hand and quickly guided her outside, where his friends were opening the glass doors to a party bus. Lights were beaming, the music was loud, and the smoke seemed to sift away through some slits in the roof. David introduced her as his new friend and stated that he wanted them all to come in to drink some wine and eat appetizers. Two of the men got out, saying they were starving, but the women all stayed in the party bus.

A bold female voice bellowed, "Let them go and eat! Go eat!"

Tina, however, was nervous and cold from the salty wind that was blowing through the alley. Her nipples were hard and since she was braless, they were rather apparent. A woman in the party bus peeked around the door as Tina was looking down, shaking her hair out to remove any remaining sand. With the music now turned down, she asked, "Are you going to hang out with the girls? We don't bite, ha-ha, we just nibble."

Tina smiled and stepped into the bus, noticing the stripper's pole in the center, as well as the women looking at her from within a smoky, spellbinding atmosphere. Three women who looked like they came straight out of a fashion magazine looked on while Tina sat down in her gray t-shirt and yellow shorts. One of the women, who exuded a strong charm, was all thighs and curved like a voluptuous violin. She noticed Tina possessed a school girl look, one of naïvete, complete with fresh skin, newly-highlighted hair, and a slender, yet cherubic face. They closed the party bus doors.

In her low, smokey tone, the violin woman said, "My name is Bianca, this is Atti and Bee."

Bee was sitting at the very back looking like an animal, whom Bianca was clearly obsessed with, as well. Bee sensually and potently directed her eyes straight into Tina's, startling her. Bee uncrossed her legs to expose herself, lowering Tina's barriers immediately. Atti fired up a joint while Bianca looked at Tina with a ravaging gaze and a sexy smirk.

At first, Tina only glanced at her sex, but then, increasingly seduced, she took a longer look. The moisture between Tina's legs immediately solidified her confidence that she could be attracted to women, something she had always suspected but never confirmed. Bee had lured her secret lesbian side out from its hiding place. As Bee walked over to Tina, the party bus lights behind her made her appear to be floating like some kind of beautiful apparition.

Bee stole a kiss from Tina before staring intently in her eye. Bianca and Atti adjusted their seating so they could watch Bee's shameless pursuit while they smoked a joint. Tina closed her eyes and gave in entirely, finding Bee's caress irresistible. Her sophisticated, possessive impulse to seduce Tina had made Tina's youthful smile blossom uncontrollably as Bee grabbed the back of Tina's hair and pushed her thick wet tongue into her mouth, almost exactly like a man's sex would have done in a different situation. Tina reached for her sex, but Bee instinctively slapped her hand away.

There was a knock on the glass doors.

"What do you want David? Go eat!"

The driver opened the doors as Bee flew quickly back to her seat.

"Oh Bianca, I love you so much girl, but please let me have Tina back now. Break the spell."

Tina smiled and walked off the party bus, all hot and sweaty.

"Are you ok?

"Yes, yes, of course, I'm fine. They're your friends."

"I know, that's why I ask."

Tina and David went back into the restaurant, where the men were engaged in conversation. The type of conversation they generated was very similar to what she heard her roommate talk like on the phone with friends. In other words, nothing Tina would likely be interested in. A constant stream of marijuana-related terms like CBG, terpenes, strains, Indica, Sativa, flower, and edibles was about all it amounted to, it seemed to her. One of the men was overly passionate about how he felt about Big Pharma and the cocktail of pills people take, since for Tina, that was an important part of what kept her calm and happy.

David noticed Tina wasn't engaged in the conversation and settled up his bill. She was now more comfortable with him and noticed something about David she had initially missed: that he was not only was fun and nice, and had exciting, wild friends, but that his throbbing heart created a pulse that she had immediately fallen into sync with. She thought about his hands running through his thick hair, his even skin. Her mood elevated as her sex began to bud.

David sensed this and asked if she would like to leave. Feeling aroused she said she had a secret at her house that he might enjoy seeing and smelling. His eyes and mannerisms revealed his heightened senses. Tina's mouth was turned upwards as she talked, implicitly inviting him to her mouth, even if elusively.

"Ready to go David?"

"I think so."

David followed Tina to her cottage. Tina, of course, would never let her roommate meet him since she would be afraid she would seduce him as Bee seduced her. Envious of her roommate's passionate manner and longing, lustful eyes, she had always been fascinated by her singular power to seduce. Tina would hear the conversations her roommate had all the time with many different men and been attracted to her moans and laughs from the other room, as she engaged in her sexual play. All the while, unbeknownst to her, Tina's roommate had admired her prudence and lofty-minded focus upon achieving success.

Tina sets up candles and pulled out a bottle of wine. Before long, the day turned to night, and Tina tired of waiting for David to make a move, so she moved closer. He let her do it willingly and, with their heads tilted down, eye to eye, they non-verbally agreed to shine a light into what up to that point, had been the darkness of mutual wonder.

"Take off all your clothes David, and lay down on your back."

"What about my wine?"

"Now!"

David's sex was rock hard and pointed straight up. She touched his penis tauntingly, making him extra-excited. Tina put on some kind of African drum music, taking off all of her clothes and straddling his face with her wet desire, right there on the floor. He ate her passionately with a circular motion, humming all the while, much like someone having a tasty delicacy. Nothing could have been more desirable to her than allowing him this moment of control over her, as he lie in the eye of her storm, directing its motions from below.

A longtime fan of threesomes, David secretly imagined another woman present while he stroked his sex and looked up at her slim, gyrating stomach. Tina's taught, yet ample behind shook and bounced tremulously, while her pubic hairs ground into his lips. She rode him rhythmically, tantalizing the clean, tart smells and tastes of her clitoris as it pressed up against his nose and tongue. Thoughts of unbridled orgies with Bee and the girls raced through her mind as seeping fluids swirled in the suction of his mouth.

Not knowing her roommate was actually home the whole time, but now hearing them clearly, Tabby snuck in an eyeful, gazing at the beauty of two perfect outlines of bodies in motion against the candlelight. His sex was raised hard and alone, causing Tabby to become roused to a fountainous degree, as she sat there squatted down behind the plants. She observed Tina smother his face dominantly, forcing both hands behind his head. The roundness of Tina's behind turned Tabby on considerably, so she walked down to her room to puts on a breast-boosting corset. She then gracefully bound her hair up with red ribbon, took a hit off her pipe, and prepared to really live the privilege of being a sexual human, of being alive. Tabby quietly tip-toed into the room of candlelight and African drum music, while the face-sitting continued, witnessing Tina squirt into David's face multiple times.

Without asking Tina, Tabby went for David's sex, giving it a slow, deep sensual caress and a lightly flickering tongue. Tina was still unaware of her roommate being in the room, lost as she was in her pelvic control of his mouth and tongue. His body shook like an earthquake, surprised and excited. Her bold move worked him up quickly, to the point that he was about to come hard, as her twisting tight grip intensified even further. David pointed his sex down from the base and exploded, yelling out as veins popped out of his neck.

Just then, Tina looked back and saw her rival, Tabby.

Tabby moved reassuringly towards Tina as she began kissing the back of her neck softly, while rubbing her breasts gently and gracefully, touching Tina's nipples, all the while feeling completely drugged due to her longstanding, yet secret attraction. Tina was shocked at first but then smiled back in her state of ecstasy.

"Is this okay Tina?" asked Tabby.

She nodded as a few teardrops fell from her eyes, in happy disbelief of how her day had gone. She released his submission to her sex as David continued to caress her.

Tina lie down on her back and signaled her roommate to get on top of her. Tabby turned in excitement toward her, with wide-open legs and her toes curled. She climbed over to her and Tina put her feet on her thighs, while David took her from behind. He was shaved and thrust into her steadily, imbibing the angelic aromas of Tabby's vagina. He also flirted with Tina, while behind her roommate, watching Tabby tremble and moan with every motion of his sex. He was excited to belong to them both in common, locked now in an infinite rotation of moisture and heat. A mixture of positions went on for hours in innumerable combinations.

Later, Tabby wanted to be in control and told him to go soft and to rub his flaccid penis on her clitoris. She whispered in his ear, "The purity of our intended natural state is that God creates Love, my Love. So, submit to my Love."

Tina's wide-eyed expression deepened as Tabby commanded him to go faster and deeper, until Tina let out a deep, grunting moan almost exactly like that of her roommate, drizzling cum profusely onto the rug. The illusion of control vs. non-control transformed into an unprecedented evening of climaxes for all three of them.

No longer clinging to the past, Tina had finally unpacked the baggage she carried around for so long and let her beauty become her arsenal. A new day of personal power had finally come, as she was no longer afraid to fail.

"Forget about this cynical and corrupt world for an hour. Take a shower, have the smoke." (DRV)

5

La Petite Mort

Rose had been living in New York for a while already when she got a phone call from an old dear friend in Washington State. Her friend was upset to find out she had cancer and that her condition was failing rapidly. Since Rose had a warm heart and loved her friend very much, she went to think things over at a nearby bar. Once she got there, she noticed a young, cute couple dressed in what appeared to be hiking clothes. They were holding each other close and drinking a pitcher of beer while watching a soccer game with friends.

(loud voice from the TV)

"Messi again!"

Rose spun in her stool listlessly, thinking about her own life and how she got to where she was at now. The bar was loud and warm. There was plenty to look at, with the walls decorated with many varieties of Americana memorabilia. After a while though, her thoughts drifted into the pains of living with her stockbroker husband Doug who had severe sociopathic tendencies. He had his face in his phone almost all the time and exhibited zero empathy for anybody.

When Rose finally got home, she didn't speak of her friend's condition to him. She was concerned about feeding his addictions to cortisol, dopamine, porn, and bragging about his own legacy, which had led him down a path in which he continually needed to win at everything. Unfortunately for her, she was a woman who positioned herself at his every beck and call. Rose felt unimportant in the relationship but thought the security and the status they shared at least looked good to her friends and family. She imagined him going away and leaving her alone, as a way to pass the time.

The big house they lived in had begun to seem very small and for Rose, became a joy to clean. Rose sometimes walked around the house singing to herself, "I wanna be loved by you" while cleaning or cooking. If she had drunk too much wine, she sometimes performed the song on top of the tables and on countertops for fun.

When she felt depressed, she would go upstairs to the bedroom, light some incense, take a small shot of liquor, put on one of his porno movies, and grab her favorite sex toy. Doug had bought her many sex toys and an armoire to put them in, with shelves and drawers.

They had met while still in college back in Raleigh, NC, at a show put on by a radio station. She had gone to the beer garden with her friends to get a drink when a charismatic-seeming young man ran into her with both of his stout beers and on his eyes, giant, silly glasses. Rose indulged him with a pale ale later on in the evening, which he told her had helped him to change his mind about his top beer preference. He saw this as a big deal since he took his own opinion so seriously.

Once they had married, the romance and adventure lasted for a while, but it turned a little dirtier, a little kinkier, a little more intense, to fulfill all of his pornographic appetites. Rose discovered much about herself as well but didn't exactly know why his controlling ways had increasingly become a bit of a turn-off to her. Soon Doug was looking outside the marriage for more fantasy-fulfilling adventures with younger and less thoughtful women. She didn't dare leave him because of all the money in the bank and the money she kept secretly stashing away for herself, even though they by that point, hadn't had sex in four years. Her masturbating rituals were bearable, but they were increasingly lonely.

The next day, Rose went to a local farmer's market and decided to walk over to what looked like a booth of greeting cards. Many of the cards featured cities like San Francisco, Los Angeles, Seattle, Las Vegas, Monterey, Honolulu. She came across an artist section of the booth and found the artists who made their own cards.

Rose grabbed one that stood out to her, which read:
"When we go from light-hearted to heavy-hearted,
There is a tax,
The mind tries to sort,
All you have packed,
So if you're unhappy and feeling,
Out of sorts,
Know I am here,
A loving support"
The message struck her to the core. Rose saw the card as an opportunity to help her friend in Washington with cancer, hopefully serving as a sign pointing towards

positive change in her life. She stocked up on her lavender soap from a local vendor, knowing that her friend would appreciate it.

Once she got home and checked for flights, she let her husband know she would be traveling to Washington to help her friend whose life had likely been shortened and who truly needed her help. Doug didn't bat an eye and kissed her on the forehead, patting her on the behind.

"When do you think you will be back?"

"Not sure."

"Who will take care of things?"

"You will Doug. You're a big boy and I'm sure you'll be fine."

A small part of her secretly saw this upcoming time as an opportunity to escape the sociopathic horrors she had undergone so many times, swallowing her pride repeatedly with each discovery of his compulsive infidelities. She wanted to heal her heart from the daily trouble in the household and the endless disputes that typically ended in a Doug-centered checkmate. She prepared for the long journey, packing all she had to live well with, including her toys. She left the next day to fly to Washington State, relieved and excited.

Rose and her friend had a good time catching up at first, but within 48 hours, the friend suddenly passed away late at night, during an intense thunderstorm. The beautiful trees and rain provided a comforting context to a vivid, mournful moment for her. Rose grieved with her friend's family and friends and gave testimony about her friend's life and impact upon her.

Once she was alone again and had collected her emotions a bit, she wondered whether she should go back to New York afterward, or maybe stay awhile to broaden her horizons, somewhere out near the majestic Mt. Rainier that had captured her attention while driving from the airport. Rose hadn't been in a position to truly be in control of her own life or actions for a very long time. She didn't want to seem insensitive to her friend's family, who she realized may have continuing needs, but at the same time, she wanted to have some type of plan.

The family called on the phone and asked Rose to stay at their place and help them take care of her friend's property until her estate was arranged. Immediately, she saw this as yet another sign that she needed to change her life. The decision to stay and help was easy to make, especially with the sunshine peeking through the clouds, illuminating the sublime mountains. She stayed at her old friend's house, fixing old doors, straightening up the pool house, organizing her old office, and hammering the gutters back in more tightly in the wake of the storm.

It was a lot of work. Sometimes she would take a break and sit in the pool house with the oversized couches, fantasizing about a different kind of man from her sociopathic husband — a caring, loving man who caressed her body and nurtured her soul. Her hand slipped down her pants with ease while the birds sang out their songs in the moving sunbeams. Her fantasy man was one who would be tall and strong and, for her, very worth daydreaming about.

Her fantasy had to come to an end though when she heard someone yelling for her from the house. In her scramble to get to it, she dipped her masturbatory hand into a fountain before arriving to meet and chat with the neighbors about what had occurred. Afterward, Rose showered and made a cocktail, while roaming the house nude. She found her friend's study with old pictures on the wall from her travels and volunteer work, and she sighed, remembering what a good person she actually was.

Later that evening, Rose grew antsy and decided to go to a local tavern a couple of miles from town. She had never really been to a tavern like this, as it was filled with loggers and older tough-looking women, as well as peanut shells strewn carelessly all over the ground. She sat down in her nice silk blouse and fancy skirt, waiting to order a drink and some food from the busy waitress.

A young man named Darren who frequented the place often walked by Rose with his red beard and dirty oily hat, flashing her a warm smile. He said, "No need to wear perfume in this place, ma'am." The only reason he had said anything at all though, was that he liked the refreshing and clean smell of a woman like her that he rarely had a chance to enjoy. Rose asked if he would like to help her polish off a pitcher of Rainier. He had never had a woman offer to buy him anything before which tickled his fancy. He sat down across from her slowly looking at the slight cleavage she seemed to have left available for him to observe. His sex thickened, though he was able to conceal it.

"Maybe you could tell me what a classy woman like yourself is doing in a place like this?"

"I came for the beer."

"You didn't come here for the beer. You know it, I know it, and everyone in this bar knows it. The last girl that came in here looking like you do, got exactly what she wanted in the back of this place with four other fellers."

"Four guys other than you?"

He paused for a moment, as she rested her chin on her fist with a strong flirting grin.

"You want to open that can of worms ma'am, go right ahead."

"Are you afraid to help me open it, young blood? Afraid you might get cut? Maybe a few more beers and you'll grow some balls."

He poured them both another beer, bewildered at her strength and confidence. He didn't know where she came from or what her story was but knew she wasn't from around their town.

A few beers later he opened up to her, expressing his dreams of traveling to Tibet and Buenos Aires. His impression of her was that she was wealthy, intelligent, and, luckily for him, obviously horny. He told her he had seen pictures from a magazine he got a garage sale of various places around the world, and that had piqued his interest. He grew more and more feverish from her brilliant wits, charm, and her intoxicated flirtations, from her eyes to her cleavage, to her posture. Darren poured some more beer and shared with her his current state of financial difficulty, which was partially due to his girlfriend stealing his money, which he kept in a box by his bed. Internally, he face-palmed himself, thinking what he said might scare her off, sabotaging the moment.

"I'm so sorry Darren. Sometimes people are just selfish and mean, aren't they? Are you working right now or do you need work?" She asked in a tone as if she had work waiting for him to do. She noticed he seem a little embarrassed and vulnerable.

In his despair, he asked her to hold on a minute, got up, and walked around the pool table to use the bathroom and be alone briefly. Rose undid two buttons on her blouse as she was increasingly intent on seducing the young man when he came back. Darren sat back down and immediately noticed her blouse was showing her tan and now, much more extensive cleavage. He began to rub his thighs without noticing it, then nervously looked up at the TV and said, "Looks like a storm tonight." She enjoyed watching his face turn red, practically gasping for air.

"Are you a strong young man?"

He felt her foot upon his leg and squinted his eyes on accident, from the unexpected pleasure. In spite of his ongoing misfortunes, his hunger for her and his disposition of kindness seemed to please this sexy older woman.

As the drinks continued to flow, playful sexual deals were made between them. Darren twisted his beard in thought, knowing the physical direction the evening was headed. Rose had become a bit tipsy and yelled in a Shakespearian accent, "Put an end to my misery young Darren, and be thy complement to my pleasure". They both laughed.

They then settled up and walked out of the tavern together, into the night. Darren opened the tavern door for Rose, politely directing her to his truck while opening the door for her to get in. She could see his strong, growing bulge and intoxicated smile. Rose knew this young man almost certainly wasn't in the back of the bar that night with the other men. His story had to be derivative of the daily bar gossip, not personal experience, since he invested it with no emotion or details. She sensed he might have gone straight from high school to the workplace and had never really been with a woman like her before in his life. Darren seemed more worried than Rose, which gave Rose a tremendous amount of comfort and control.

Darren drove his old pickup drunk while following

directions from Rose, both of them laughing at every pothole in the street and missed turn. When they arrived at the house, Rose took Darren by the hand and walked him through the side gate to the pool house. She playfully spanked him for driving drunk and made him promise to never do it again while laughing.

Darren agreed laughingly too, before gazing over at the manicured lattice-enclosed porch to the pool house.

"Let's go inside before it rains."

Her voice remained steady upon the perfect tone and pace she knew could intoxicate any man. She turned the thermostat up to ninety-five degrees in the pool house to warm up the brilliant red and gold marble floors and to prepare for a hot-and-sweaty evening. She slithered out of her dress and blouse slowly and put on a small, classy bikini, right in front of Darren.

"You don't seem to be afraid of anything, are you?"

"My husband trained me not to be afraid."

"You're married?"

"Well of course Darren, but he is thousands of miles away and I am in the mood to play. Are you in the mood to play, young man?"

She put on trancey techno-type music she had gotten into when she lived in New York, as she headed slowly over to the hot tub. Darren laughed nervously. She fantasized about what she might want to do with him and how she could addict his soul with ecstasy, movement, and dance. As the plot thickened in her mind and her sex grew moister, she reached down to touch it, telling him to prepare. Darren was so excited he didn't want to take off his pants, knowing his member would be sticking straight up. He sat in a childish ball of shyness and anguish.

Rose let out a sigh and said, "Relax Darren, let's smoke a joint."

Darren walked over to her by the wet bar to take a hit and accidentally grazed her with his hardened cock. The nymphs of his imagination seized him amidst whistling winds, a powerful woman of apparent rulelesness and vice, and an artistically-designed roach clip. The grass tasted like pine and as it affected him more, propelling his desire to truly live in the moment.

"What is this Darren?" she said while tapping the top of his member and jolting suddenly between her thighs.

"Perhaps you need a whiskey."

Darren went to grab the whiskey from Rose, as Rose teasingly pulled away. She signaled him to drop to his knees and began to pour the poison into his mouth, holding his chin. She put the bottle down and looked into his face. His eyes were closed. She snatched up the bottle of whiskey and poured another drink as though she had done this before, knowing it was taking effect.

She moved quickly to take off all of his clothes, laughing at the poorly-constructed knots on his boots. Rose quickly pulled him to the couch and jumped on top, spitting on her hand to slicken her tingling, gaping pit of desire. He squirmed like sizzling meat on a grill when her tongue descended down upon him. Rose softly pet his cock with her sex. She straddled him and fluttered kisses around his nipples. He jolted. She placed his sex inside of her and brought her legs together, forcing his legs into a reverse straddle. She climbed up to one foot and shaped his legs into an Amazon position, putting herself fully in control of the sex. Stumbling over his now-scattered emotions, he belonged to her in this drunken, hot, wet moment as she drove her frustrations down, down, down into a vortex of pure ecstasy. He whimpered as she growled, reversing the conventional gender roles. A violent, unexpected storm descended upon them and rain poured down on the metal roof of the pool house, pattering with a vengeance. Pure energy and madness grew more and more powerfully deep into the hot night. After a long day of work and endless orgasms, Darren couldn't stand it anymore and simply fell asleep.

Around midnight, Rose was getting her second wind and was clearly in control of the evening as she surely didn't want it to end. She got up from Darren's arms, got up off the couch, set up aromatic candles, and begins to rub his feet with Eucalyptus oil.

"These feet seem so tired."

Darren woke to a Eucalyptus-like smell and his feet being rubbed. He laughed and said, stunned, "I can't believe this."

Darren stood up over Rose, ready to prove himself a man, and noticed the room seemed prearranged. She did not hesitate in her finest garters and lingerie she had changed into, for her new intimate friend.

Rose said, "You need a thousand dollars and I need a screaming orgasm". Shocked, Darren was taken back by Rose, because her sex drive was extremely high and considerably wild.

"Take this pill and get to work on my fetish, love. We still have a long rich night of fucking ahead of us."

Although her confidence seemed powerful, he still had a small bit of worry about how or if the evening would unfold to her liking. The shadows danced around the room in a dance of lust.

He was a strong one and sexed her until he hurt. He lost himself in the tiny, raging fire within her. Two hours after midnight, Darren's penis had had enough and he felt horrible that he couldn't go on to satisfy her cravings, as he'd been rubbed raw.

"Not to worry Ginger man, you will get your thousand dollars in the end."

She brought in an ensemble of toys and oils in a hand-carved box. Rose handed Darren her favorite toy and spread her sex, knowing her time had come. He looked to her a bit like a child, with a look on his face of curiosity, discovery, and exhaustion. Taking possession of her fancy, she helped induce the fountain of passion from her desire, with quivering limbs, fluttering eyes, and a magical mixture of taboo and assertiveness. His tongue flickered like a hummingbird spirit that had fluttered down to play upon her clitoris. The thunder and lightning were startling and at the moment intensified the electric sexual momentum they'd built up. Both overwhelmed by the corruptions of nature and toys, she drew out her frustration, his anger, her hurt, his passion, her wrong, his right, and made the night sing, until they both practically fainted into sleep. There lay the carnage of the evening all over the pool house, as Darren savored the taste and smell her wild fruits, and awakened, as they lightly lay in the debris of climax around them.

"Make me a resident of my own free spirit." (DRV)

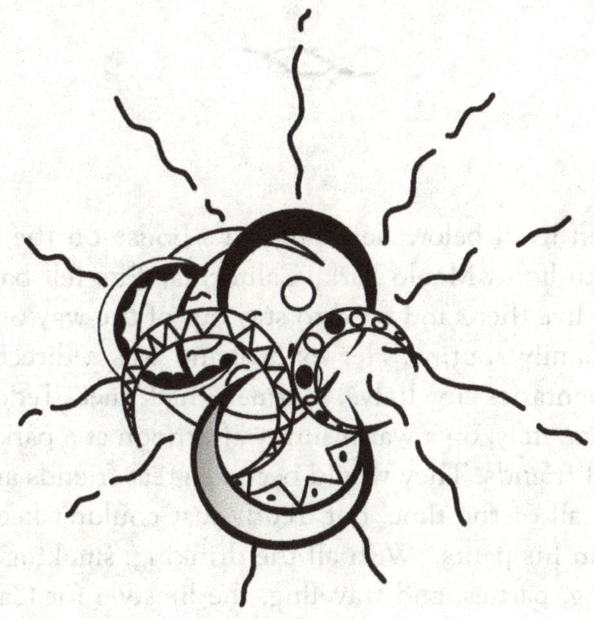

6

Boy Toy

Carmen lived below her daughter's house on the lower level studio in Menlo Park, California. She felt bad she had to live there and tried to stay out of the way of their daily family routine. Her ex-husband was a director of documentaries in Italy. Carmen had met Teddy in Cosenza, Italy, on a warm sunny afternoon at a park with mutual friends. They would become great friends and go sailing all of the time, but Teddy just couldn't keep his penis in his pants. With all the drinking, smoking, boat hopping, parties, and traveling, the lifestyle for Carmen was fun and adventurous, albeit with a constant hint of danger.

The rush she got from it came from not knowing what was coming next. After a while though, the parties started to feel stale: all the same people, same brags, same atmosphere, just different settings. The chapters of their lives started to feel like the chapters of some old Bible. On top of that, the lifestyle was too haphazard to easily keep a marriage together for both of them. As time went on, Carmen and Teddy divorced, albeit somewhat civilly.

Time passed fast. They had been divorced three years before she moved to the United States with her daughter. Something had been broken inside of her that she couldn't get back, but there seemed to be a positive path unfolding that she was determined to follow.

Carmen's daughter had a house that overlooked the Bay Area, featuring panoramic windows with a full view, spanning the length of the house. Their family worked hard and they had many nice things, but culturally, it was difficult for Carmen to understand the gluttony of their lives, the language they used, and the habits they had grown used to on a daily basis.

Carmen never said much. She was more of an observer and didn't ever stir the pot in the household out of respect and out of her own philosophy of life. The feeling to Carmen was that she was in their world and clearly the studio downstairs was where she fit into it. Her loneliness ran deep, and in ways that they couldn't see. Her experience was that of an older culture, but she was fine with it.

Carmen jumped in her convertible one day, gathered up some beach items, and head out for Half Moon Bay. It was a beautiful drive, about twenty miles over a large hill to the beach. She set up camp just below the cliff in the hot morning sun, taking a small puff on what she called her "sneak-a-toke." Carmen had the type of skin that tans easily as she begins to darken, her tan lines vibrant and beautiful. She had an older body, but she looked like she had never been overweight.

After napping a bit, Carmen got up to grab a container

of fruit when a much younger man approached her with confidence beaming through his eyes and lighting up his sexy smile. He was a mixed-ancestry American mutt, beautifully put together. There was no telling where he was from or why he possessed such a powerful glow.

He said nothing at first, so Carmen said, "Would you like to sit down and have a piece of fruit?"

He said, "Yes I would."

He was still a young man and loved taking chances. He had seen Carmen's beauty from far away and was even more excited to find that she was also an older woman. Carmen and Bobby flirted back and forth for a while. Bobby kept looking at her petite, loose breasts, excusing his gaze by saying he was looking at her beautiful tan lines, but Carmen knew what he was doing. She got up and took off her top like she was in her own bedroom. He was shocked but didn't move as she put on the sexiest see-through shirt he had ever seen. His desire to see this unfolding through to the end had solidified. Carmen was flattered by Bobby because, in her eyes, he was a beautifully sculpted young man with considerable potential left in his world. Carmen asked Bobby how old he was, to which he replied, "Old enough. But listen. The truly beautiful day starts with how your heart speaks to you, and how I speak to you."

"You are full of surprises."

"So are you."

She smiled, waved him over to follow her, and headed up the trail to her car with Bobby. She took him to a nearby restaurant on the wharf and ordered for both of them, choosing appetizers and a fine bottle of white wine. Bobby got excited and became enlivened. He ran across the street telling her he'd get her a bunch of ranunculi. While he was gone though, she saw his wallet and fingered his ID. He came back in a hurry, and was proud, as if he had acquired the catch of the day. Bobby sat down and handed Carmen the flowers.

"Did you steal those? You left your wallet."

"No I didn't steal these – I'm trying to charm your heart a little. Do you like the flowers?"

"I do."

"Thank you."

"No, thank you."

Carmen's disguise was coming off, as she continued absorbing his intentions.

He went on talking about his favorite movies, showing off his attractively well-worn, yet still-young appearance. While he was talking, Carmen found herself slipping into fantasies about him, while moisture quickened between her legs. She was flattered by his presence and energy towards her, so she tortured him with erotic questions, arousing his curiosity for the still-unknown between them.

Her pheromones, now increasingly apparent to his senses, hypnotized him as they passed over his nostrils. Every now and then, she would pinch his cheek once firmly, with each flattering remark he gave her. The erotic tension was peaking more and more with every sip of wine and touch. She trained him with her relentless, seductive questions until he was completely enamored with her foreign air and grace.

Carmen insisted on paying for the bill at the end and they drove her convertible to her studio. His sex was hard the whole way and Carmen could see his legs shaking and stimulating his erection, though she did not comment right away. She put some contemporary jazz on the radio and watched Bobby close his eyes and enjoy the wind upon his face.

"You must really like convertibles Bobby", she said, as she pointed to his sex.

Bobby didn't seem to care as he smiled and continued to throw his head back into the warm summer day. Carmen kept looking down at his sex and became a little nervous inside. She imagined reaching down and petting it, even while driving. The scenes produced by her mind were dangerous, as she wasn't watching the curvy road in front of her, but imagining undressing him instead.

"Are you ok to drive Carmen?"

Carmen was going too slow on the highway and cars began to honk, throwing the mood completely off for her, so she went faster and looked down to see if his sex was still erect. Bobby caught Carmen looking at it.

"Do you want to see it, Carmen?"

Bobby pulled out his thick sex and wagged it for her.

"You are going to make me crash Bobby stop!! Oh my God!"

Bobby laughed and put his penis back in his pants.

"You want to see it again."

"You are bad Bobby and no I don't. Why are you so hard Bobby?"

Her accent drove him wild and he began to pet his sex with persuasive power. Carmen reached over and lightly pet his sex, momentarily transported to a place of a more untamed desire.

"Strong penis Bobby, you are a strong young man."

Carmen considered the morality of righteousness and sin that potentially stood in the couple's way, but was not dissuaded.

They arrived at her studio on the hillside and she told

Bobby to make himself comfortable as she headed straight to the bathroom for a shower. He heard her lock the door but tried the knob anyway. He was burning with youthful desire and couldn't imagine why she would lock the door. He felt a sense of rejection and betrayal, not to mention a bit teased. He knocked loudly on the door, hoping she would answer. Carmen just ignored, taking her time, knowing the locked door would only heighten his flame. Feeling challenged by Carmen, he prepared himself for the possibility of total rejection by upping the ante.

Just then, she came out as he lay naked on the couch with Italian Opera playing on the record player. This seemed reasonable to him, given the chain of events leading to her place. But she got upset, briskly walking across the room, carelessly rocking her breast out of her kimono, before slapping him. Her fragrance was of coconut oil lotion and the beach they had just come from.

"Turn around", she said sternly.

Her kimono was completely wide open and her sagging tan-lined breasts were still wet, oily, and shiny. Carmen then pulled his arm, turned him around, and spanked him fast and hard on his behind.

"The audacity!" Carmen said while running out of breath.

"Why are you doing this to me? Am I old Bobby? Do you want to make Love to me Bobby? Huh? Do you?!"

Face-to-face in obvious, mutual ecstasy, he spun her around and down into the bean bag, entering her hot, loose desire. His penis was thin and pumping slow at first to adjust to her levels, but then moved very fast as she became wetter and wetter. The sexualized odor in the air was strong as his lean body angled itself to lightly rub her g-spot with each passing pump. He tightened his stomach muscles and began to rail into her, as she asked him to slow down as she moaned. She felt ravaged and boiled over into an erotic frenzy, as she deliberately took a plunge into the unknown.

She started to moan louder, feeling a powerful, unforced orgasm coming. Her roaring, animalistic sounds made Bobby pump even faster.

She screamed into a pillow, "I'm coming!!"

With a moan, he slowed down and looked at her face, pausing over her like a heavy-breathing Saint Bernard, wondering what foreign rituals might explain the obscure style of her orgasm. He was able to bring her to the height of ecstasy within minutes, which he never thought possible with any woman he'd been with before.

Slipping in their sweat and fluids, exploring each other's bodies, he said, "Don't worry, I am close. "

Carmen rolled her eyes and embraced Bobby's sex with her vagina with all of her might. Slowly stirring again, he rolled her sideways and touched her clitoris this time. She moaned then listened closely to the sound of his penis sliding in and out of her. He softly rolled his fingers in a circle on her side as she bit his shoulder and dug her nails into him.

His gestures and movements were brilliant in their sensuality. She moaned and came quickly again and again, as he scissored her legs and penetrated her again from a new angle. Playfully, she cursed at him over and over, in a spitting, sweaty, restless climax. She was exhausted and crying tears of joy. She moved slowly to roll and reach over for a glass of water that was on the table.

Tenderly, Bobby stopped and picked her up to take her into the shower where he washed her back, legs, feet, and body for her. She loved his soft touch and relished in his understanding, care, and empathy towards her.

Carmen very much wanted to please Bobby in return, so she took his penis and balls deep into her large mouth. She had him pinned to the wall of the shower, to his disbelief. Her mouthfeel and the grip of her cheek and tongue were tender and perfect. She rubbed his behind and he came in seconds. She stroked him between her breasts as he moaned harder than he ever had. She made love to his cock with the underside of her breast until he came again and sunk to the floor in the depths of orgasm. They washed and dried each other off, and he put her in bed where she fell asleep as Bobby looked on, amazed.

Unsettled by his emotions, Bobby walked outside and ran up the stairs to the street, hoping to recover his senses. The beauty and uniqueness of the moment had propelled him to drop his boundaries, allowing him to be consumed by her charming, exotic elegance.

Carmen's daughter from the main house came out and said, "Where do you think you're going without a shirt stud?"

She brought him inside where she asked if he would like something to drink. She sat him down.

"Plans today? I need help in my garden and I'll need you too, young man."

Bobby said nothing.

The daughter continued with a wry smile, "So uh, I heard you met my mother."

"To be what we want to be, To see what we want to see,
To perceive the way we want, To perceive the life we
breathe, the sex we need." (DRV)

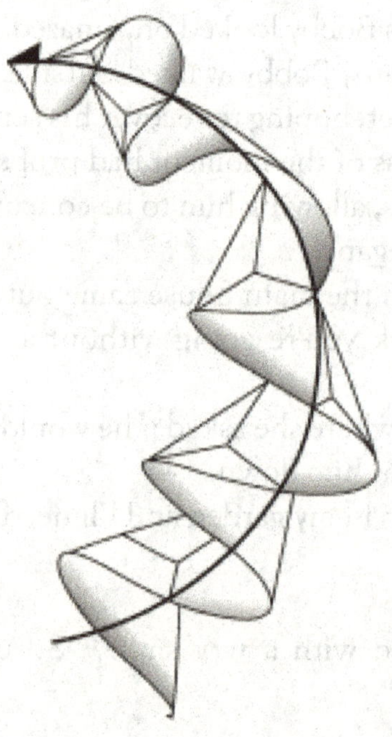

7

Blind Date

"My bullshit detector must be seriously off," Olivia thought to herself.

Every time she decided to work on a relationship, things would fall apart. She had many great friends, but they were all women that were either mad at men in general or were with a man trying to create an impossibly ideal successful relationship. Her grandparents were a decent example of how nice a marriage can be, but nobody ever fully warmed up to her grandfather, having been from the mainland and enlisted in the Navy many years ago. He had lived in Hawaii most of his life. He remembered Pearl Harbor and how the attack affected the island and the islanders.

Although she was Native Hawaiian, Olivia was still a relatively sheltered girl: her dad made good money, while her mom's side of the family was heavily into Hawaiian sovereignty and were aligned with what they called the

Aloha Spirit. Sometimes on the weekends when she was younger, she would be made to stand outside of the military bases with signs telling the military to go home. This was normal to Olivia, and afterward, the local families would all get together for a luau together.

One time when they were having a small bbq at her cousin's house down the road, her friend brought over a Marine with a couple of his cute young friends. This did not sit well with her aunt, but her uncle insisted it was going to be okay and that this would be an opportunity to reflect the Aloha Spirit. By then, all of her cousins had surrounded the young men, glaring at them. All at once, the young Marines fought their way out of their situation, running down the beach. The Hawaiian cousins couldn't keep up with them and a large discussion followed back at the bbq about Hawaii, its history, and its relation to the US Military, in pidgin.

The only thing was, Olivia didn't feel the same way as her aunt did, nor was she nearly as angry about it. She was really just looking for love with a type of man who was soft and sweet, but also able to protect her even from her cousins' and family's anger.

She was a big woman with strong hands, a sexy smile, and a gentle soft-spoken character. Although Olivia had been through a lot, she also knew there must be a man out there who she could love sweetly and gently, like a child. Every Hawaiian man she had ever met was not of that nature and so in some respects, she became prejudiced against her own culture.

She sought a type of man, in her mind, who would be child-like, with needs of softness, understanding, and nurturing, but also strength. She had an idea of what kind of man she wanted physically that in some ways, actually conflicted with her ideals. He had to have muscles, a tan, a sweet smile, responsive eyes, a soft grip, and a love for children, since she hoped to have some one day.

One day while Olivia was out shopping at the local store, she ran into a young man with almost all of these attributes and his presence was like a magnet to her.

"Hey."

"Hey."

"I've seen you around."

"Oh yeah? I've seen you too."

They started off just having a soft-spoken conversation, which slowly grew into more pronounced flirtation. Trying not to, he would still end up looking down at her cleavage between her bikini top. His semi-erection became impossible to hide and Olivia got a good eye full of his powerful member. Both of their mouths were open in shock as he waited for her to move, acutely aware of what they both knew was rising in him. Elevated and spiritually bound, neither one feared a thing.

Not wanting to be too forward though, she asked him to hang out with her at a local karaoke bar for some drinks and food — needless to say, they didn't stay long. Olivia realized this wasn't altogether the safest thing to do, hanging out with him, but in her mind it was simple. She imagined explaining to her friends later, "He was soft with a cute friendly smile, a new convertible car, and a decent singing voice. What can I say? We liked each other."

She told him she knew of a really nice beach nearby where they could hang out and talk. They walked down the beach and he admitted to her that he was always gone on operations in other countries, so he tried not to get into any serious relationships. She saw him looking at her cleavage every now and then though, with his hands in his pockets, and she knew that wasn't his true preference.

They laid down a blanket and enjoyed each other's caresses as the sun went down. She reached down to his still-small penis and began to massage him. His inexperience was exciting to her as she took off her pants and panties, and climbed on top of him. The warmth of the Hawaiian night enhanced the resonance between them. He couldn't take his eyes off of her breasts jiggling around with their long, hard nipples. He took his penis out of his pants and put it into her. Olivia went to take off her shirt and her breasts dropped out of the bottom of the suit. His sex moved effortlessly into her until he let out a deep grunt and stopped. Unfortunately, this would be both the beginning and the ending of her relationship with this young man.

Months later she discovered she was pregnant and of course, she quickly knew who the father must be. She had found out through his friends at the bar who he was. He never knew she was pregnant, and she never told him, but not because of him, because of her own family.

While talking to her friend Kayla on the phone, Olivia got an offer to have a babysitter for a night so she could get out and do something. Olivia bubbled over with excitement and was so touched to receive the babysitting gift, but didn't know what to do with it. Kayla said she could set her up with this charming construction guy who was working on her deck. He had asked Kayla the week before if she knew a girl that might want to go out with him.

"It would be perfect", Kayla said.

"How do you mean?"

"Well, he's single and is kind of soft-spoken like you."

"Yeah, but what if he finds out I have a baby?"

"Girl, take a look at your jugs. They are huge sista. Make him crawl to you and make him want to be with you. You know?"

"I do?"

"Just, just, just take him out. I would if I weren't married."

"Have you been watching him?"

"Girl, he is strong sista, and hard working. You try."

Kayla called Michael the next day and set up the date at a local Italian restaurant for him and Olivia to meet. Michael was nervous but decided he was going to dress up for Olivia anyways, thinking to himself that just maybe, she could help to dissolve his loneliness and be the treasure of the partner he had been looking for.

Michael put on tight jeans to show off his strong legs and butt, which paired well with his strong, virile face. He was tired of seeing his friends kissing and walking around with smudged lipstick on their faces, while he had no one to be close to. He normally dated pretty girls that were far more beautiful than most of theirs, but they were admittedly, few and far between.

Olivia was excited too, but worried he wouldn't like the fact that she had a new baby. She put on a low-cut dress to show off her newly-oversized milky breasts and vermilion lipstick. She did her best not to allow herself to establish some abstract ideal for what he should look like, but the reality she was setting up for herself was nerve-wracking all the same. She called Kayla for advice and asked her for a ride to the restaurant.

When Olivia and Michael met up at the local Italian restaurant they were both immediately attracted to one another. Michael tenderly pulled out her chair and his eyes dipped, discretely, to her chest. He ordered a bottle of wine to loosen things up a bit. Michael told Olivia that he was a hard worker in construction and that in reality, he was pretty simple-minded, usually quiet, but in good shape. He continued that he was also a passionate person, but that he was kind of scared of women since his girlfriend had left him for a lead singer in a band.

"She was so cold to me. I was in her world and then... I wasn't"

Olivia was quiet and could hardly believe her ears. Inside she kept stumbling over his openness and honesty, hoping he wouldn't be too scared off when she broke the news to him about her baby. The heavenly aroma of the steaming cioppino, an Italian seafood garlic stew, permeated the table area as they looked at each other happily, smiling through the steam. Olivia kept drinking the wine but didn't touch her food.

Michael asked, "Something wrong?"

"I just had a baby."

"Oh! Wow. Congratulations."

Olivia kept looking for a scared look as she began to eat her meal. But Michael continued to smile happily at Olivia. He was perfectly fine with her baby. Both were fantasizing about the possibilities, given how well it was going. He was impressed with her courage and her honesty, especially to be willing to share some basic facts that she thought of as an imperfection.

The mood in the restaurant grew warmer and more romantic when he gathered up his courage and touched her hand. His provocative glances twisted something deep inside of her, unlocking an erotic craving. Her heightened desire for pleasure was able to develop further, given the counterbalance her strength offered to his weakness. As she unconsciously brushed her bosom and took another sip of wine, Michael stiffened uncomfortably in his tight pants.

They finished their meals and drank the rest of the wine. Olivia told him she knew of a downtown underground club she had always wanted to go to, but never could. Michael said he was completely down for some adventure with a swallow and a glance, finding the situation completely refreshing as they continued into the night.

Olivia then took him to the underground club, located in a dark part of Chinatown where, with him by her side, she knew she would feel safe and able to let loose. She would finally get to dance away the everyday turbulence of motherhood with a man of her dreams. The club was downstairs from the street level and you could hear the bass booming from the outside. This was the type of club Michael would never go to, filled as it was with fog and disco lights, but he was willing to experiment.

Olivia seemed to be moving in slow motion while Michael's perception adjusted to the atmosphere. They did a shot and a beer and before long, began to dance relentlessly. This seemed almost tauntingly cruel to Michael as he noticed Olivia had put glitter on her cleavage that hadn't been there before. Olivia was instantly familiar with his touch and they both knew the fire has been lit as he tried to adjust his erection, accidentally revealing his engorged state of being. He couldn't help but to look at her sparkly, love-potioned cleavage in the strobe lights, along with the bold twinkle in her eyes. She brought him under her spell, watching him gazing in awe at her billowy bosom. Double shots were then ordered by each of them, while she continued to seduce him gently. An overall aura of mutual temptation hung in the air as Olivia brushed across his sex with increasing frequency, lightly pulling his hands towards her twists, turns, and bumps throughout the night.

Unable to take it any longer, Michael ran to the bathroom stall to masturbate, since he was about to burst, but he was distracted by loud obnoxious drunks and had to stop in mid-stroke. When he came back out, Olivia said she wanted to show him this wonderful beach she liked to sit and read at sometimes. Michael agreed, escorting Olivia to his car, where she guided him to a fancy part of the island where he hoped to find a secret place they could make love.

The new-age monk music they were playing reverberated loudly in the warm night air through his sunroof as they look out at the moon, deftly aware of what awaited them if they so chose. As they approached the beach, she found an oversized towel along with a picture on the floor of the car. The image was of Michael on top of a mountain. She looked at it and delicately kissed the picture, foreshadowing the evening to come. The wait seemed perpetual, but he knew they'd be there soon.

"Can we use this towel to sit on Michael?"

"Sure, it should be dry. We went spearfishing the other night and caught four fish. We blackened them the next day and put it in a Caesar salad."

"Oh, you like to cook?"

"There are two things in my family that we love to do; one is to cook. The second is to build stuff. Started out just with birdhouses and dog houses, but I just kept building my whole life, and well, here I am."

"Here you are!"

"Yep here I am and here you are."

"Ha ha."

"Turn down here and park in front of that beach access sign."

They arrived. Olivia loved his smell and his pleasant overall vibe. He was confident even while vulnerable. She had remembered what her friend told her and wasn't going to let this one get away.

They were so mutually giddy that they were almost skipping down to the beach after they got out of the car. The trail featured a Hawaiian ti leaf impressed into the square pavement pieces that passed between two large homes to the secluded beach. The waves broke softly and the water was still warm on their way. They found her favorite spot under a welcoming tree, where they could sit on the towel and see the moonlight through the branches on this romantic, quiet night. Olivia wasted no time in laying him down, lightly kissing his cheek. Michael felt her soft lips on his cheek and began to kiss her back. Their soft tongues slid over each other while Michael wrapped his arms around her body.

Pleasuring talk and dirty whispers ensued, as they'd been repressing it all night long:

"You've been tied up in knots tonight, haven't you? I want you to know my care for you is selfless and sweet. You are perfect to me. Is your care for me selfless and sweet too, Michael?"

"Of course it is."

"Are you sure Michael?"

Gazing at Olivia's sparkly cleavage he froze up and repeated, "Please.....please.....pleease."

She pulled down her shirt and placed her milky breast into his mouth, fulfilling the hunger of sexual healing that his long hours, construction lifestyle so often precluded.

Her nipples were large and erect, and Olivia felt it pulling down his throat as she squeezed her breast to entice him. The waves broke softly, whispering to the two foreshadowings of what was near.

Olivia wanted so badly to love and to be loved. With her nurturing heart, she welcomed this caressing man lovingly, while gripping his cock tightly. For a moment, she wanted to make sense of the complexity of feelings and thoughts, but watching his body move simply left her in a state of now-purified desire. As he continued to worship her breasts with his mouth, he felt as if he was dreaming, and with his eyes closed, he began drinking her milk. The weight and the softness of her fleshy breasts smothered his face easily.

"You'll have to suck harder."

"I'm getting full."

He squirmed his head out of her bosom to try to get away, even while she moved to pin him down in the sand. She squeezed her nipple to squirt his face and then put her breast into her own mouth. Her warm wet thick tongue and luscious plump lips calmed him down as he placed her other bosom into his mouth. Her hand slid down his face, his chest, and to his fully erect sex fully. She tapped it at first to watch it bounce and began to stroke it through his tight pants.

Suffocating once again in her ample breast and its milk, he spat it out, panting.

"Hold on."

She lay her body sideways on his arm and held his wrist down above his head in a completely enveloping embrace. She lightly massaged his sex, while looking into his eyes. The pain of constriction became unbearable in his tight jeans, but he persisted nonetheless. The sensation was intoxicating as the pair swayed together in a heavenly embrace under the Hawaiian moon. They kissed each other lightly, slowly, spiritually.

Olivia sat up and pulled both breasts out of her lace bra, caressed them, and began stroking him harder. Michael tried to stand up to take his pants off of his body and to avoid an embarrassing climax, but he was too late. Her single, then double grip, made him come intensely, right in his tight pants. He let out a yell and fell to the ground, gripping the sand as he let her caress him more, accepting the fate she'd dealt him.

Olivia was a goddess to him, and he resigned his spirit to their love once more. Her sex was buffered and moist as he lie still in her arms, waiting to gather his senses so he could offer her his mouth. He imagined kissing her feet and then slowly walking his kisses up to her sex. With his eyes closed, he heard waves crash lightly on the beach. When he opened his eyes again, the moon was shining off the water, and he realized he was now alone, with only a note from her as his new companion under the slowly rising sun.

"Gather up the thoughts, put them in a bag, take a ride." (DRV)

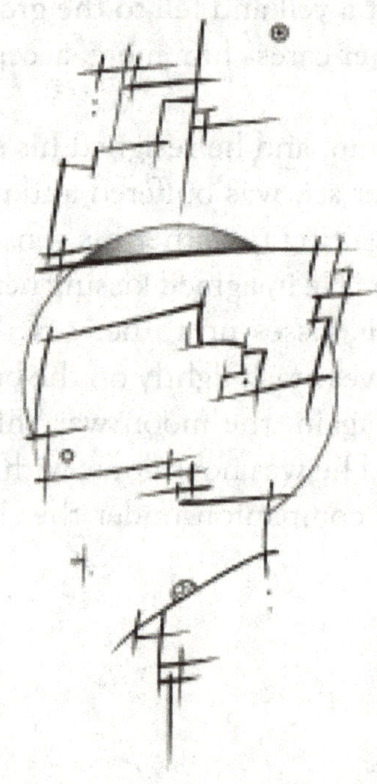

8

DJ and Bae

Daniel and his girlfriend Elle were living in an apartment near Westwood in Los Angeles. His intuition had told him before they moved into the apartment that something was a bit off, that a dark cloud seemed to hover over them, but money was tight, so they went for it. He had started to work for a bagel place down the street because it was the first job he could find near the apartment. His girlfriend Elle didn't need to work because her parents were well-to-do. To make ends meet, Daniel had started to DJ for a club too, in addition to the bagel place.

His girlfriend was high maintenance and was pursuing an acting career. She would leave for long periods in the middle of the night with her foolish actor friends who seemed to believe everything she said. He had a hunch why she was always gone so much, but, he wouldn't want to open a can of worms that he could not handle. Elle was beautiful, worshipped, and intimidating. Though Daniel was stylish in his own ghettoish manner, he would not fit into this crowd. All the same, he adored the elegant, chic Elle whom he called his girlfriend.

They had met in Santa Cruz some years back while attending the university. A mutual friend was going to a drum circle and was handing out magic mushrooms to those tagging along. They all squeezed into a van and headed to the park on a sunny afternoon near the ocean. The drums swelled in their hearts. The feeling of light and beautiful love pervading the music filled its sounds, movement, and rhythm. The gyrations of their hands and arms felt poetic and bohemian. Elle and Daniel had to share a drum. Elle watched Daniel's muscles tense up after he took his shirt off since he was starting to sweat. The masculine aroma was strong and unpleasant at first but would actually act as an aphrodisiac to her, as the drumming pressed on. Elle closed her eyes at one point exploring the possibilities of leaving behind her family's expectations and simply pursuing the many sexual secrets she had never been able to before, but had always wanted to. Daniel was lost in a trance, believing Elle's vibrations made him vibrate the drum. The mushrooms completely opened up everything in his consciousness.

They dated for a year, partied with mutual friends, and graduated in the same class. Daniel loved being the center of attention with his DJing skills and crazy outfits. Elle joined in with her costumes and loved being on the microphone to keep things goings at their themed parties.

Elle had her heart set on Los Angeles while Daniel had already affirmed he was going to go wherever she wanted so they could be together. Daniel was the type to always land on his feet and in this context, to help weather the storms that Los Angeles would bring to their lives. He knew this city would be a test for both of them, being so young and adventurous.

One night, Elle got drunk at the club Daniel was DJing at with her friends and began what seemed to him her "mating call" dance. She was being rude to Daniel, shouting and embarrassing him in front of her friends, taunting him about him working at a bagel shop and the consequent smell of his clothes. He wondered why he should have to behave and be the understanding guy for her when she acts like such a mean and abusive fool.

In this very moment of clarity, Mercedes, a black woman, walked up to request a song with tattoos on her neck and a bottom-row gold tooth. Mercedes tried to work her specific angle into the club's atmosphere with her ongoing music requests because she loved the club so much and loved the control of the beat. She started making song requests over and over with a light booty tap to Daniel, while leaving out Elle. Mercedes was aware of what was going on between them through their body language and so she decided she would side with Daniel. He smiled from ear-to-ear and played every song she wanted.

In the dark, she took his hand and said, "I kinda like you, white boy".

Daniel sensed this seemingly nice and sweet, yet also thoroughly hardcore black mama possessed an air of control. He delighted in her mysterious looks that roused and stirred him in places he had never thought of. An innocent, tender kiss on the cheek from her had not seemed so innocent at all, but rather more of a smoldering, intoxicating kiss delivered in a slightly sinister, slow-motion manner. She was sexy and she knew it.

Mercedes had never been with any boys other than

black ones. Daniel fit the description of what she thought her future might hold for her someday, in that he was tall and intelligent, amongst other qualities. She recognized a resonance in her heart with Daniel which was his commitment to a true sense of equal love. Elle to her was just a meaningless blip in his life and her intentions were to lure him out of it. Underneath Mercedes' hard exterior was an intelligent, wise woman on a private journey to claim poetic justice.

Mercedes told him everyone was meeting at her suite at the hotel afterward and that he should show up to DJ the party. She then disappeared into the crowd.

After she did, Daniel found a napkin in his pocket that read, "I'll be back for you." The club closed late in the evening and Elle was now nowhere to be found. Daniel was unplugging his equipment when he saw Mercedes come back from the party to meet up with him.

"I can't find my girlfriend," he says.

"She is already at my party, DJ".

She left a trail of desire for him through the wet street lights and pervasive shadows to the hotel. Mercedes offered a protective force field that was alluring to him, despite being a little drunk. Because she had never felt the vibe of someone like Daniel, she was confused about whether to be sexy and flirt directly or to move more slowly. The smile and twinkle in Daniel's eyes were captivating and continuously inviting despite her uncertainty and evasiveness.

He was quiet and watched her struggle in a multitude of rushing feelings. The badass attitude she had portrayed slowly melted away and her guard was tenderly set down to rest, for the moment. Daniel felt as if her deliciously attractive ways held a much deeper meaning. He adored her chuckles and the brief reach for his hand she attempted. She was sincere in the telling of her desires, which intertwined effortlessly with his sensitive demeanor and his stories. Not once did Daniel even dream of someone who had the fortitude and poise to listen and care for him as she did. She puts her finger to his lips.

"We are here now and I hope you're ready for all this."

"I was born ready Bae."

She laughed.

She took his hand and guided him through the lobby and to the elevator. The suite was crowded and a DJ was already playing. Mercedes excused herself and went over to a group of her friends by the wet bar. Daniel strolled across the room and grabbed a wine bottle off the table. His plan was to be cool with his girlfriend and to score points for finding this grandiose party, but she was already submerged in flirtation with an older man by the balcony. Daniel went into the bathroom and as he did, a group of hoity-toity fashion girls who were with Elle at the club snickered, laughed, and left while looking over at Daniel.

"Bagel-man," one sneered loudly.

His heart skipped a beat. He felt like he looked like a jackass and considered going home, so he washed his face and pushed his hair back to calm his nerves. When Daniel came out of the bathroom, Mercedes was waiting for him and gave the girls with Elle the stink-eye.

"You ready boy?"

"Ready for what?"

The smile that suddenly came over him was a 180-degree turn from his earlier sense of humiliation, and he could see himself from Elle's point of view, as a triumphant sense of pleasure beckoned them both. Mercedes grabbed his hand in front of everyone and towed him into the master bedroom before locking the door. Daniel has about one single second to completely understand her intentions while he took in a panoramic view of the room. She smiled in a friendly manner and he mirrored her. He was confident now that she was in this moment of his life to untangle the knots of humiliation and confusion that had accumulated in his heart, his mind, his life.

Daniel was fully invested in this, so he smiled, and sat down on the bed, asking, "Do you want to wrestle Bae?"

"Oh, is that what you and your girlfriend do."

"Nope."

He couldn't stop smiling as they wrestled hard and rolled around, and around, and around. Breathlessly and disheveled, Mercedes lept up and started pouring shots on top of the dresser. They laughed and poked fun at Elle and her friends. Elle heard them laughing through the door and began to knock. She swore she would leave him if he didn't open the door and come out. Amazed and delighted to hear the breakthrough in her voice on the other side of the door, they giggled with even greater intent.

Mercedes dropped to her knees and tenderly pulled down his sweatsuit pants and put his small wilted penis in her mouth as he grew, licking, sucking, pleasing him while Elle asked through the door for a ride home.

With a broken voice, he said, "I can't help you right now, bye."

"What am I supposed to do?"

Mercedes said with a moan,

"Figure it out and leave."

Elle screamed.

Daniel performed a little jig with his arms and hands and looked down at Mercedes, realizing that this was going to be a complete shedding of the past. He was tender to her with his touch, a touch Mercedes had never known until his sparkly-eyed stare and light-hearted ways challenged her tough upbringing, which had been one of street survival. Mercedes half-suspected he would dis her later, but for now, the pure sensation of the moment and the circumstance shot a beam of light into their mutual darkness.

Mercedes swung his slender body into her arms and to the bed, to break his embrace. Her strength and violent movements shocked him with pleasure and paralyzed his thoughts. She had powerful curves and stretch marks that captivated him. Her breasts fell onto him as she rubbed her moisture onto his sex while throwing off her wig. The mystery of her persona kept his blood pumping, while her large round nipples were soft and the tips long and hard, rubbing against his face. She breathed on him like an animal preparing her prey, before his penis entered her with his legs together, as she squeezes her desire and legs on to him from above.

He could only hope to sustain such a mutually charged experience while pinned down, but it wasn't clear that he could without her guidance. Closing his eyes, he felt as if he had slipped into a giant bowl of wet noodles, completely naked. Reaching, grabbing, slipping endlessly, poking, soaking in sweat, every move they shared remained deeply pleasurable and unpredictable. Her countless long orgasms were as wet and warm as a tropical ocean as she rode him selfishly and powerfully.

When a knock at the door arrived once again, she smiled and said, "Relax DJ, I got this."

"Understanding is more grey than black and white."
(DRV)

9

The Longing

Gene was at the flea market one late sunny afternoon in San Jose's autumn season. He was a tall Spanish man, well-groomed and nicely dressed on the daily. The vendors knew him well and treated him with respect. The market was loud and crowded that day, with families and dealers. Suddenly, he felt his back pocket wiggle, only to find a Spanish teenaged girl trying to pickpocket him. He turned and grabbed the wrist of the arm holding his wallet. He noticed though, that she was completely unafraid. In fact, she was practically seething sexual energy through her eyes, in a manipulative, smirking manner. At the same time, she also looked rather hungry, slender, sunburned, and scared.

Gene looked down at her, took back his wallet, and asked if she needed some food. She nodded her head. Gene walked her to the food stand for a tamale, where she ate like an animal. Her dirty black hair, worn-out, skimpy clothes, and filthy hands belied her condition, but she was radiantly beautiful, all the same. She was fresh-looking in her own way and the alertness in her eyes was contagious.

Gene said in his thick Spanish accent, "You're sure hungry."

He bought her a second tamale and asked her if she had a warm place to sleep tonight. She stopped chewing and shook her head.

Gene waited for her to finish the other three tamales he bought her and then they headed back to Gene's house. His intentions were pure: to help this teen who was on the streets and who could use a good night's sleep. Gene made her agree that there would be "no monkey business". She didn't speak much but agreed, despite seeming desperate and unsure of the nature of the situation. Survival was her game. Gene looked over at her. Her eyes told a story he knew he could never understand. As she looked out of Gene's car window, living in the moment, she was, at least, delighted to move in a positive direction, even if only for a day or two.

When they arrived, Gene told her to go in the bathroom and shower. Gene's condo was straight-laced, contemporary, and clean. He loved plants and candles. He had a roommate, Phil, but he wasn't home at the time. Sometimes he would be gone for days on end, due to his job at the airlines. Phil was a local, tall, sensitive man who was typically too shy to ask women out, but people always loved him and his gentleness.

Gene found some old shirts and sweat pants for her to wear. Instead of asking questions, he decided to himself, he'd just be an empathetic good guy, and make her a bed on the couch, now that the day had melted into the night.

He cracked some wine and she walked out with nothing

on. She was tan with prevalent tan lines and small teardrop breasts with large soft nipples.

Gene said, "Let me get you the shirt and sweats".

She said, "No."

Gene's sex slightly hardened and little chili peppers of heat under his skin began to redden his face. Speechlessly, he watched her float towards him. Gene was hypnotized, knowing this teenage flower was reserved for someone else, but she was now standing before him.

Gene said, "I don't even know your name."

She said, "Mary."

She moved in close and bumped his sex with the back of her hand, which sets his stiffening process into overdrive. At just that moment, who walked in but Phil, frozen in his steps at the front door. He seemed more embarrassed than they were and speed-walked down the hall, covering his eyes. They both laughed and the mood changed. He gave her the shirt and sweats and excused himself to go to bed. He told Mary they would talk more in the morning.

Phil later walked into the kitchen in PJs to get something to drink, passing Mary on the couch. Mary sat up and looked at Phil. He looked over and meekly smiled, waving at her. He noticed her beauty and how confident she was, now sitting Indian-style on the couch.

"Are you comfortable on the couch?"

"Maybe"

"Are, are, are you staying the night?"

"Maybe, are you shy or something?"

In a dash, Phil bolted to his room. She was excited to make Phil feel this way because she was used to men clawing at her like a bear. The thought of gentle hands had always excited her, but she seemed to attract the animal-like men who were selfish and would just toss her little body around into different positions. Her ability to intimidate men was normal to her and manipulation seemed the only way to survive, on top of stealing and robbing.

Phil felt his sex fill with desire as he arrived in his room breathless. He decided to leave his door open just a crack, as his fantasies coming from having a young woman in the house took over. He lay in bed erect, with his fingers positioned into a ring of her tight sex. He massaged the head of his penis and took long strokes down to the base, thrusting up with his hips. Phil believed she might be the perfect complement to his shy nature.

At that point, Mary got up and knocked open Gene's bedroom door, rather than Phil's. She wanted to thank him for the day and night and wanted to apologize for trying to steal from him. Gene asked a few questions now that she was being more open and found they had a lot in common when it came to art and fashion. Mary was older than he thought. Gene lit some candles in his room and brought in the wine he had corked earlier. They both laughed and drank into the deep night. Phil jealously listened from the next room and decided to put on his headphones. He fell asleep.

Gene and Mary fell asleep together and she awoke in the dark of the early morning looking for her pants. She pulled a joint out of the back pocket of her jeans and laid back down with Gene. Gene woke up to the smell of the marijuana in his bed. Mary was lying on her back, hitting the joint. She passed it to him, while Gene looked over at Mary, smiled, and decided he must try it. Mary jumped on top and straddled Gene to shot-gun his smoke. With bloodshot eyes, his member grew as Mary twisted to tenderly rub it with the heel of her hand. She told him to take his pants off while pinching his nipples. She then took him in. Phil woke up to the sound of moaning coming from Gene's room. He listened for hours on end, trying to imagine it was him in Gene's place. It was an orgasmic morning for everyone.

By morning light, they were all in the kitchen for coffee and Gene said he must catch his flight out and that Mary could stay if it was ok with Phil. Phil agreed. Needless to say, nothing could prepare Phil for what the day had in store for him.

After breakfast, Gene left and Phil asked Mary nervously if she would like to go on a hike at a nearby park. She blushed at Phil which made him shake like a leaf and replied,

"Ok Phil, I'll hike with you, I hope we can bring food."

Mary enjoyed his squirming. She took off her hoodie and asked Phil for another shirt. Phil sprang to his room, slammed the door, and anxiously rubbed his sex. He receded back into his fantasies earlier that morning of being in Gene's place with Mary. The orgasm wasn't coming fast enough, so he grabbed his lube and squeezed harder. He finally got his erection fully angled and primed for release. She could hear his light sounds of stroking as she leaned into the crack of his closed door. Mary smiled and knocked at the door. Ashamed, Phil tried to quickly fix himself and fell down. He got up and walked over to his dresser to grab an undershirt, cracking the door and holding out the shirt for Mary.

"Here! I have to gather the things."

Phil grabbed some grapes, crackers, cheeses, and water at her request. Her youthful teen smile was captivating as she nonchalantly hugged him from behind in a loving embrace, while he packed the food.

On the way to the park, Phil saw a women's store in the downtown area and decided to buy Mary an outfit because it was a little cold out. He took pleasure in buying her clothes and delighted in his slight view into the slit of the curtain of the dressing room. Mary would come out periodically looking for approval in her upscale dresses. Full of compliments, his desire became engorged several times over, as he knew she wasn't looking for anything warm. He admired the lightness of her being and her true innocence.

Her tiny teen breasts would slightly bounce as she spun around in her dress.

"We'll take the dress and some shorts for the hike."

Her skin was so even and darkly tanned. Her tan lines stood out around her petite shoulders and back. She thanked Phil over and over again. She hugged him for a long time and kissed his neck. He loved her, but was careful and didn't dare show signs of attraction, as he kept Gene's probable reaction on his mind. They strolled light-footed from the town to the trail as if they were on a cloud.

Her new outfit was alluring and perfectly matched her flow. She was skipping and dancing in her brand new duds along the trail as she flirted and even spanked Phil on the butt to watch his cheeks cherry. He could sense she had never known a real orgasm and he wondered the same about himself. He wondered if there may be more to it than he had thought. Equally curious about one another, they slowed down to an opening off the trail, and laid down a blanket, nestled and hidden. In soft golden tall grass, they sat and Phil pulled out a pocketbook from his bag that was full of love poems. He asked if he could read his favorites to her. Mary agreed and laid down on her side, holding her head up with her hand:

"An affectionate hand,
Helps to understand,
The struggles in us all
Heart pound on the same beat,
I repeat, Hearts pound on the same beat,
I know my quiet fire glow will burn her to a crisp,
If she can handle it all, being wealthy in patience,
Then maybe my heart wouldn't seem so translucent."
Mary smiled.
"One more."
"Bounce, bounce, bounce me off the walls of your eternal Love,
In many beauties, I've been tossed in the rocking chair of life,
Musing weather play hide and seek, or to play life slow.
I tiptoed on the forsaken trails of demons
and now I will give my utmost freshness to the wild fields of Love.
Can I dance and move with lissome grace, as I put my hand upon your face,
and flop on top to sing the melody of lovemaking?"
The soft warm sunlight beamed through the branches while the birds chirped in the distance. Phil and Mary shared food, wine, and fun stories from their childhoods. Now that the wine was gone, the warmth of the day had made the atmosphere more lazy and relaxed. They napped together and embraced. After a long while, Mary began to act like she was sleeping but was, in reality, peeking at his sex, gazing at his penis outline through his shorts, fascinated by her natural instinct, despite him being a different type of man. She begged for it quietly inside as her hunger grew, and she caressed his stomach.

He saw her eyes seduced by his penis, "Amused by what you see?."

He made her overcome her inexperience with the charm of a sweet gentleman. He ran his hands through her hair and softly pet her cheeks. He melted her with kisses to her neck and nibbles to her ear. Phil unzipped his shorts and stopped. Softly, she opened her legs, an earthly splendor.

He said softly, "Am I too old to take you, Mary?

In a playful nervous act, Phil grabbed his book next to him.

"It says here in the book:
'Time and experience is life's golden fruit,
Careful with ambition, you might overshoot.'
Am I overshooting Mary?"

A flock of birds flew low and passed by as the tree cast shadows upon their bodies. He discovered her moisture through her panties and her new shorts. He took them both off while doing everything he could to keep her buried in his soft kisses. She made up her mind to close her eyes and submit fully to Phil. He made magic circles with the utmost gentleness and persistence upon her body, his fingers were careful and gentle. Her body convulsed.

His long, flickering tongue stiffened the clitoris and the touch of his finger made her moan. She trembled and bloomed thoroughly under Phil's caresses, in the heat of the autumn sun. Phil muttered to himself his desires and intentions. She rolled on top of Phil and the wind began to blow her black hair to the side as the leaves landed softly all around. The moment was angelic. They rolled into the blanket to stay warm and ground their pubic hairs together. The lube was still on Phil's penis from earlier that morning. Her sex was tight and angled his penis to an electric sensation, sparking and roaming throughout her whole body.

"Slow down Mary, or I am going to come."

Phil's request was obviously going to be ignored, as the posturing of her body and hips suggested determination and momentum. She ground the cum out of him and continued to ride harder until he was soft once again. She then moved slowly and gently off of him.

They fell asleep again, but within an hour, Mary awoke to the coldness of the near night and gusting winds. The sky was dim and she felt she must run, to return to her independent life. While she grabbed her bag and headed down the hill, Phil woke up and told her to wait for him. He packed up the poem book and the blanket, but it took him a minute to find Mary while running down the hill. There were four trails that branched off the main trail, he realized, as he slowed down to take a look down each one. He finally reached the main road and looked back with confusion, thinking "I may never see her again."

"I'd exhaust my sacred fragrance all over her body and endure the patience to grow and love once more." (DRV)

About the Author

David Vercauteren is a forward-thinking author and artist based in the Seattle metropolitan area. He is the founder of Philosatees and has worked as a manager and trainer in the cannabis, music, and cell phone industries. Vercauteren's next book of erotica will serve as a follow-up to this one.

Contact: drv1974@yahoo.com